SCIENTIFIC AMERICAN EXPLORES BIG IDEAS

Understanding the Bond Between Humans and Pets

The Editors of *Scientific American*

SCIENTIFIC AMERICAN EDUCATIONAL PUBLISHING

New York

Published in 2024 by Scientific American Educational Publishing
in association with **The Rosen Publishing Group**
2544 Clinton Street, Buffalo NY 14224

Contains material from Scientific American®, a division of Springer Nature America, Inc.,
reprinted by permission, as well as original material from The Rosen Publishing Group®.

First Edition

Scientific American
Lisa Pallatroni: Project Editor

Rosen Publishing
Michael Hessel-Mial: Compiling Editor
Michael Moy: Senior Graphic Designer

Cataloging-in-Publication Data

Names: Scientific American, Inc.
Title: Understanding the bond between humans and pets /
edited by the Scientific American Editors.
Description: First Edition. | New York : Scientific American Educational Publishing, 2024. |
Series: Scientific American explores big ideas | Includes bibliographic references and index.
Identifiers: ISBN 9781725349575 (pbk.) | ISBN 9781725349582
(library bound)| ISBN 9781725349599 (ebook)
Subjects: LCSH: Human-animal relationships–Juvenile literature. | Animal
behavior–Juvenile literature. | Domestic animals–Juvenile literature.
Classification: LCC QL85.U963 2024 | DDC 591.5–dc23

Manufactured in the United States of America
Websites listed were live at the time of publication.

Cover: Sinseeho/Shutterstock.com

CPSIA Compliance Information: Batch # SACS24.
For Further Information contact Rosen Publishing at 1-800-237-9932.

CONTENTS

INTRODUCTION

Humans aren't meant to be alone; we're social creatures, who need the community of others to be truly ourselves. But that community extends beyond the human species. For thousands of years the animals that hunt our mice, herd our sheep, and populate our folklore have become something more: our pets, who we dote on and treat like members of the family. In this title, we'll learn about many different animal species we invite into our homes.

Pride of place goes to dogs and cats, whose wild ancestors evolved into their domestic form through human intervention. Section 1, "Our Close Bonds with Cats and Dogs," explores that long relationship. Along with these animals' evolutionary history, we learn some quirks of their anatomy, as well as the right and wrong ways to care for them. Sections 2–"Exploring How Animals Communicate"–and 3–"Animal Psychology and Behavior"– debunk the idea that animals are completely mindless. Animals have sophisticated communication systems with a lot of variety. They form abstract concepts, coordinate their activities through consensus, and can be reasoned with–if we know what gestures or sounds they best respond to.

Section 4, "Quirks of the Human-Pet Bond," illustrates how humans are changed by their relationship with animals. We all have animals for different reasons. In this section, we'll learn the psychological effects of cuteness, what happens when we have to surrender pets, and how our pets were impacted by the COVID-19 pandemic. The final section, "Other Pets in Our Lives," touches on more obscure pets, some of which bring additional costs of pet ownership. The section celebrates the unsung ferret, and explores ecological problems caused by the exotic pet trade.

Nothing quite captures the memories we form with our companion animals. They're family, after all. But in these articles, you might find a mirror of your own relationship with a pet, or better appreciate the bonds people form with animals you'd previously overlooked.

Section 1: Our Close Bonds with Cats and Dogs

Why Do Cats Purr?

By Leslie A. Lyons

O ver the course of evolution, purring has probably offered some selective advantage to cats. Most felid species produce a "purr-like" vocalization. In domestic cats, purring is most noticeable when an animal is nursing her kittens or when humans provide social contact via petting, stroking or feeding.

Although we assume that a cat's purr is an expression of pleasure or is a means of communication with its young, perhaps the reasons for purring can be deciphered from the more stressful moments in a cat's life. Cats often purr while under duress, such as during a visit to the veterinarian or when recovering from injury. Thus, not all purring cats appear to be content or pleased with their current circumstances. This riddle has lead researchers to investigate how cats purr, which is also still under debate.

Scientists have demonstrated that cats produce the purr through intermittent signaling of the laryngeal and diaphragmatic muscles. Cats purr during both inhalation and exhalation with a consistent pattern and frequency between 25 and 150 Hertz. Various investigators have shown that sound frequencies in this range can improve bone density and promote healing.

This association between the frequencies of cats' purrs and improved healing of bones and muscles may provide help for some humans. Bone density loss and muscle atrophy is a serious concern for astronauts during extended periods at zero gravity. Their musculo-skeletal systems do not experience the normal stresses of physical activity, including routine standing or sitting, which requires strength for posture control.

Because cats have adapted to conserve energy via long periods of rest and sleep, it is possible that purring is a low energy mechanism that stimulates muscles and bones without a lot of energy. The durability of the cat has facilitated the notion that cats have "nine lives" and a common veterinary legend holds that cats are able to reassemble their bones when placed in the same room with all their parts. Purring may provide a basis for this feline mythology. The domestication and breeding of fancy cats occurred relatively recently compared to other pets and domesticated species, thus cats do not display as many muscle and bone abnormalities as their more strongly selected carnivore relative, the domestic dog. Perhaps cats' purring helps alleviate the dysplasia or osteoporotic conditions that are more common in their canid cousins. Although it is tempting to state that cats purr because they are happy, it is more plausible that cat purring is a means of communication and a potential source of self-healing.

About the Author

Leslie A. Lyons is an assistant professor at the School of Veterinary Medicine at the University of California, Davis.

What You Don't Know About Your Dog's Nostrils

By Julie Hecht

Nostrils. Your dog has them. Two of them actually. And you don't give them any attention, do you? Sure, you might take your dog to the vet when you see gunk coming out of them, but on any given ho-hum day, you're not giving your dog's nostrils a second thought.

Of course, we all know I'm being entirely unfair. What more attention could you possibly give to your dog's nostrils? There they are—one, two. To get a detailed sense of what your dog's nostrils are up to, you can't just eyeball it. Even researchers can't eyeball it—instead, they videotape a dog's nose and then analyze nostril activity frame-by-frame.

Marcello Siniscalchi and colleagues from the University of Bari and the University of Trento in Italy are behind this excellent figure. I assure you, they weren't trying to get close-ups of dog faces or recreate a beam-me-up, take-me-to-your-leader scenario. The video camera attached to a cotton swab with different odors helped the researchers investigate whether dogs use a particular nostril (the right side or the left) when investigating different smells. While there are many ways to discern how dogs interpret the different stimuli they encounter every day, nostrils could be another (albeit probably less expected) way in.

Here's what happened in the study: 30 mixed-breed dogs were presented with six different odors a number of times. The odors were chosen because they differed "in terms of familiarity and emotional valence"—including some things dogs would be gung-ho about, others not so much. The six odors were the smells of 1) dog food, 2) vaginal secretions from a healthy female dog in oestrus, 3) lemon, 4) a swab with nothing on it, 5) sweat from a known veterinarian, and 6) adrenaline. You can imagine that a dog might be pretty interested in the first two odors and find them nonaversive. On the other hand, the smell of a known veterinarian and adrenaline could be more noxious (although vet visits certainly don't have to be noxious. And visit the end of the post* for how the smell of a veterinarian was put on the cotton swab).

Over the course of a few weeks, the dogs smelled the different scents a number of times, and essentially voted with their nostrils. When presented with the potentially noxious stimuli (the vet and the adrenaline), dogs "showed a consistent right nostril bias," meaning they started investigating with the right nostril and stayed investigating with the right nostril over subsequent presentations. On the other hand, when presented with potentially nonaversive stimuli, like the food and the vaginal secretion, dogs initially investigated with their right nostril and then shifted to their left.

Although dog nostril research (if you want to call it that) is in its infancy, this difference in nostril use is something to write home about as it could indicate something about a scent's valence (novel or familiar; positive or negative) as well as how scents are being processed in a dog's brain. The researchers describe the olfactory neural pathway to the brain—"in mammals the olfactory system ascends mainly ipsilaterally, with most receptor information from each nostril projecting, via the olfactory bulb, to the primary olfactory cortex in the same hemisphere (Royet & Plailly 2004)." Essentially, what goes in the right nostril is being processed on the right side of the brain, and what goes in the left nostril goes to the left side. Lateralization research suggests that the right hemisphere is often involved in investigating novelty and is also associated with "intense emotions, such as aggression, escape behavior and fear," while the left hemisphere is more focused on routine investigation and categorization, approach behavior, and positive emotional valence. The researchers' findings are consistent with those general principles. Dogs tended to begin their investigation of the different scents with their right nostril (novelty), and they continued to investigate the potentially arousing stimuli—like the vet odor and adrenaline—through the right nostril. But over repeated presentations of nonaversive stimuli—like the food and smell of another dog—dogs switched to the left nostril.

Did you already get out the video camera to start taping your dog's nostrils? I completely understand. Do I want to know which nostril dogs use when they first meet me? Of course I do. Do some dogs jump in with the left nostril while others start with the right? And if so, when do they switch to the left? So many nostrils, so little time.

Notes

* How to put the smell of a veterinarian on a cotton swab: "The veterinarian was instructed not to use deodorant/antiperspirant for 2 days before the experiment ... and to take only a shower on the morning of the experiment. On the day of the collection, the cotton swab was placed under the armpits of the vet for 10 min and then stored at -80 C until testing (several samples were collected)."

Want more on lateralization in dogs? Here you go: The authors of this study have a chapter in the recent edited volume, *The Social Dog*, 2014. Eds. Kaminski and Marshall-Pescini. Over at *Do You Believe in Dog?*, Mia Cobb covers research into other methods to assess laterality in dogs.

The views expressed are those of the author(s) and are not necessarily those of Scientific American.

About the Author

Julie Hecht is a Ph.D. student studying dog behavior and writes the Dog Spies blog at ScientificAmerican.com.

Why Cats Taste No Sweets

By David Biello

S ugar and spice and everything nice hold no interest for a cat. Our feline friends are interested in only one food: meat. This predilection is not solely the result of an inner killer just waiting to catch a bird or torture a mouse. It also occurs because cats lack the ability to taste sweetness.

The cause has been traced to a gene. The tongues of most mammals hold taste receptors—proteins on the cellular surface that bind to an incoming substance, activating the cell's internal workings and leading to a signal being sent to the brain. Humans enjoy at least five kinds of taste buds: sour, bitter, salty, umami (or meatiness) and sweet (as well as possibly fat). The sweet receptor is actually made up of two coupled proteins generated by two separate genes: *Tas1r2* and *Tas1r3*.

All cats, however—including lions, tigers and British longhairs, oh my!—lack a chunk of DNA that occurs in the *Tas1r2* gene of other mammals. As a result, the depleted feline gene (more properly called a pseudogene) does not code for the proper protein and thereby prevents cats from tasting sweets. "They don't taste sweet the way we do," says neurobiologist Joe Brand, former associate director and now member emeritus of the Monell Chemical Senses Center in Philadelphia.

Brand and his colleague Xia Li discovered the pseudogene about 12 years ago, when they followed up on decades of anecdotal evidence of cats' being sweetness-impaired, such as cats showing no preference for sweetened over regular water.

Of course, there are also plenty of anecdotal accounts pointing in the other direction: cats that eat ice cream, relish cotton candy or chase marshmallows. "Maybe some cats can use their [*Tas1r3* receptor] to taste high concentrations of sugar," Brand says. "Or perhaps they are cuing on some other compound that we cannot appreciate."

Scientists do know, however, that cats can taste things we cannot, such as adenosine triphosphate (ATP), the compound that supplies the energy in every living cell. "There isn't a lot hanging around in meat, but it's a signal for meat," Brand says. Plenty of other animals have a different array of receptors, Li says, from chickens that also lack the sweet gene to catfish that can detect amino acids in water at nanomolar concentrations. "Their receptor is more sensitive than the background concentration," Brand notes. "The catfish that detects the rotting food first is the one that survives."

Cats are not alone. Brand and his colleagues have since found that all felines (some 36 species) and several other species of strictly meat-eating mammals all lack a sweet receptor. Cats may also lack other components of the ability to enjoy (and digest) sugars, such as glucokinase in their liver—a key enzyme that controls the metabolism of carbohydrates and prevents glucose from flooding the animal's bloodstream.

Despite the cat's inability to handle sugar, most major pet food manufacturers use rice or other grains in their meals. "This may be why cats are getting diabetes," Brand offers. "Cat food today has up to 20 percent carbohydrates. Cats are not used to that—they can't handle it." What these fearsome predators of suburbia cannot taste may be hurting them. But it also means that most cat lovers don't have to worry about Kitty snatching their unattended dessert.

About the Author

David Biello is a contributing editor at Scientific American.

How House Cats Evolved

By Carlos A. Driscoll, Juliet Clutton-Brock, Andrew C. Kitchener, Stephen J. O'Brien

The aloof and elusive nature of cats is perhaps their most distinctive feature, endearing to some and exasperating to others. Despite such mercurial tendencies, the house cat is the most popular pet in the world. A third of American households have feline members, and more than 600 million cats live among humans worldwide. Yet as familiar as these animals are, a complete understanding of their origins has proved elusive. Whereas other once wild animals were domesticated for their milk, meat, wool or labor, cats contribute virtually nothing in the way of sustenance or work. How, then, did they become fixtures in our homes?

Scholars long believed that the ancient Egyptians were the first to keep cats as pets, starting around 3,600 years ago. But genetic and archaeological discoveries made over the past 15 years have revised this scenario—and have generated fresh insights into both the ancestry of the domestic cat and how its relationship with humans evolved.

Cat's Cradle

The question of where domestic cats first arose has been challenging to resolve for several reasons. Although a number of investigators suspected that all varieties descend from just one cat species—*Felis silvestris*, the wildcat—they could not be certain. In addition, that species is represented by populations living throughout the Old World—from Scotland to South Africa and from Spain to Mongolia—and until recently scientists had no way of determining unequivocally which of these wildcat populations gave rise to the tamer, domestic kind. Indeed, as an alternative to the Egyptian origins hypothesis, some researchers had even proposed that cat domestication occurred in a number of different locations, with each domestication spawning

15

a different breed. Confounding the issue was the fact that members of these wildcat groups are hard to tell apart from one another and from feral domesticated cats with so-called mackerel-tabby coats because all of them have the same pelage pattern of curved stripes and they interbreed freely with one another, further blurring population boundaries.

In 2000 one of us (Driscoll) set out to tackle the question by assembling DNA samples from some 979 wildcats and domestic cats in southern Africa, Azerbaijan, Kazakhstan, Mongolia and the Middle East. Because wildcats typically defend a single territory for life, Driscoll expected that the genetic composition of wildcat groups would vary across their geographical ranges but remain stable over time, as is observed in many other felid species. If regional indigenous groups of these animals could be distinguished from one another on the basis of their DNA and if the DNA of domestic cats more closely resembled that of one of the wildcat populations, then he would have clear evidence for where domestication began.

In the genetic analysis, published in 2007, Driscoll, another of us (O'Brien) and their colleagues focused on two kinds of DNA that molecular biologists traditionally examine to differentiate subgroups of mammal species: DNA from mitochondria, which is inherited exclusively from the mother, and short, repetitive sequences of nuclear DNA known as microsatellites. Using established computer routines, they assessed the ancestry of each of the 979 individuals sampled based on their genetic signatures. Specifically, they measured how similar each cat's DNA was to that of all the other cats and grouped the animals having similar DNA together. They then asked whether most of the animals in a group lived in the same region.

The results revealed five genetic clusters, or lineages, of wildcats. Four of these lineages corresponded neatly with four of the known subspecies of wildcat and dwelled in specific places: *F. silvestris silvestris* in Europe, *F. s. bieti* in China, *F. s. ornata* in Central Asia and *F. s. cafra* in southern Africa. The fifth lineage, however, included not only the fifth known subspecies of wildcat—*F.*

s. lybica in the Middle East—but also the hundreds of domestic cats that were sampled, including purebred and mixed-breed felines from the U.S., the U.K. and Japan. In fact, genetically, *F. s. lybica* wildcats collected in remote deserts of Israel, the United Arab Emirates and Saudi Arabia were virtually indistinguishable from domestic cats. That the domestic cats grouped with *F. s. lybica* alone among wildcats meant that domestic cats arose in a single broad locale, the Middle East, and not in other places where wildcats are native.

Once we had figured out where domestic cats came from, the next step was to ascertain when they had become domesticated. Geneticists can often estimate when a particular evolutionary event occurred by studying the quantity of random genetic mutations that accumulate at a steady rate over time. But this so-called molecular clock ticks a mite too slowly to precisely date events as recent as the past 10,000 years, the likely interval for cat domestication. To get a bead on when the taming of the cat began, we turned to the archaeological record. One find has proved especially informative in this regard.

In 2004 Jean-Denis Vigne of the National Museum of Natural History in Paris and his colleagues reported unearthing the earliest evidence suggestive of humans keeping cats as pets. The discovery comes from the Mediterranean island of Cyprus, where 9,500 years ago an adult human of unknown gender was laid to rest in a shallow grave. An assortment of items accompanied the body—stone tools, a lump of iron oxide, a handful of seashells and, in its own tiny grave just 40 centimeters away, an eight-month-old cat, its body oriented in the same westward direction as the human's.

Because wildcats are not native to Mediterranean islands other than Sicily, we know that people must have brought them over by boat, probably from the adjacent Levantine coast. Together the transport of cats to the island and the burial of the human with a cat indicate that people had formed special, intentional relationships with cats nearly 10,000 years ago in some parts of the Middle East. This locale is consistent with the geographical origin we arrived at through our genetic analyses. It appears, then, that cats were being tamed just as humankind was establishing the first settlements in a part of the Middle East known as the Fertile Crescent—the Cradle of Civilization.

A Cat and Mouse Game?

With the geography and an approximate age of the initial phases of cat domestication established, we could begin to revisit the old question of why cats and human beings ever developed a special relationship. Felids in general are unlikely candidates for domestication. The ancestors of most domesticated animals lived in herds or packs with clear dominance hierarchies. (Humans unwittingly took advantage of this structure by supplanting the alpha individual, thus facilitating control of entire cohesive groups.) These herd animals were already accustomed to living cheek by jowl, so provided that food and shelter were plentiful, they adapted easily to confinement.

Felids, in contrast, are solitary hunters that defend their home ranges fiercely from others of the same sex (the pride-living lions are the exception to this rule). Moreover, whereas most domesticates feed on widely available plant foods, felids are obligate carnivores, meaning they have a limited ability to digest anything but meat—a far rarer menu item. In fact, they have lost the ability to taste sweet carbohydrates altogether. And as to utility to humans, let us just say that our cats do not take instruction well. Such attributes suggest that whereas other domesticates were recruited from the wild by humans who bred them for specific tasks, ancestors of domestic cats most likely chose to live among humans because of opportunities they found for themselves.

Early settlements in the Fertile Crescent between 9,000 and 10,000 years ago, during the Neolithic period, created a completely new environment for any wild animals that were sufficiently flexible and inquisitive (or scared and hungry) to exploit it. The house mouse, *Mus musculus domesticus*, was one such animal. Archaeologists have found remains of this rodent, which originated in the Indian subcontinent, among the first human stores of wild grain from Israel, which date to around 10,000 years ago. The house mice could not compete well with the local wild mice outside, but by moving into people's homes and silos, they thrived.

It is almost certainly the case that these house mice attracted cats. But the trash heaps on the outskirts of town were probably just as great a draw, providing year-round pickings for those felines resourceful enough to seek them out. Both these food sources would have encouraged wildcats to adapt to living with people; in the lingo of evolutionary biology, natural selection favored those wildcats that were able to cohabit with humans and thereby gain access to the trash and mice.

Over time, wildcats more tolerant of living in human-dominated environments began to proliferate in villages throughout the Fertile Crescent. Natural selection in this new niche would have been principally for tameness, but competition among cats would also have continued to influence their evolution and limit how pliant they became. Because these proto–domestic cats were undoubtedly mostly left to fend for themselves, their hunting and scavenging skills remained sharp. Even today most domesticated cats are free agents that can easily survive independently of humans, as evinced by the plethora of feral cats around the world.

Considering that small cats do little obvious harm, people probably did not mind their company. They might have even encouraged the cats to stick around when they saw them dispatching mice and snakes. Cats may have held other appeal, too. Some experts speculate that wildcats just so happened to possess features that might have preadapted them to developing a relationship with people. In particular, these cats have "cute" features—large eyes, a snub face and a high, round forehead, among others—that are known to elicit nurturing from humans. In all likelihood, then, some people took kittens home simply because they found them adorable, giving cats a singular foothold at the human hearth.

Why was *F. s. lybica* the only subspecies of wildcat to be domesticated? Anecdotal evidence suggests that certain other subspecies, such as the European wildcat and the Chinese mountain cat, are less tolerant of people. If so, this trait alone could have precluded their adoption into homes. The friendlier southern African and Central Asian wildcats, on the other hand, might very well have become domesticated under the right conditions. But *F. s. lybica* had the good luck of proximity to the first human settlements. As agriculture spread out from the Fertile Crescent, so, too, did the tame scions of *F. s. lybica*, filling the same niche in each region they entered—and effectively shutting the door on local wildcat populations. Had domestic cats from the Fertile Crescent never arrived in Africa or Asia, perhaps the indigenous wildcats in those regions would have been drawn to homes and villages as urban civilizations developed there.

Rise of the Goddess

We do not know how long it took to transform the Middle Eastern wildcat into an affectionate home companion. Animals can be domesticated rapidly under controlled conditions. But without doors or windowpanes, Neolithic farmers would have been hard-pressed to control the breeding of cats even if they wanted to. It seems reasonable to suggest that the lack of human influence on breeding and the probable intermixing of proto–domestic cats and wildcats militated against rapid taming, causing the metamorphosis to occur over thousands of years.

Although the exact timeline of cat domestication remains uncertain, long-known archaeological evidence affords some insight into the process. After the Cypriot find, the next oldest hints of an association between humans and cats are a feline molar tooth from an archaeological deposit in Israel dating to roughly 9,000 years ago and another tooth from Pakistan dating to around 4,000 years ago.

Testament to full domestication comes from a much later period. An ivory cat statuette from Israel, more than 3,200 years old, suggests the cat was a common sight around homes and villages in the Fertile Crescent before its introduction to Egypt. This scenario makes sense, given that all the other domestic animals (except the donkey) and plants were introduced to the Nile Valley from the

Fertile Crescent. But it is Egyptian paintings from the so-called New Kingdom period—Egypt's golden era, which began nearly 3,600 years ago—that provide the oldest known unmistakable depictions of full domestication. These paintings typically show cats poised under chairs, sometimes collared or tethered, and often eating from bowls or feeding on scraps. The abundance of these illustrations signifies that cats had become common members of Egyptian households by this time.

It is in large part as a result of evocative images such as these that scholars traditionally perceived ancient Egypt as the locus of cat domestication. Still, even the oldest Egyptian representations of wildcats are 5,000 to 6,000 years younger than the 9,500-year-old Cypriot burial. Although ancient Egyptian culture cannot claim initial domestication of the cat among its many achievements, it surely played a pivotal role in subsequently molding the dynamic of domestication and the spread of cats throughout the world. Indeed, the Egyptians took the love of cats to a whole new level. By 2,900 years ago the domestic cat had become the official deity of Egypt in the form of the goddess Bastet, and such cats were sacrificed, mummified and buried in great numbers at Bastet's sacred city, Bubastis. The sheer number of cat mummies found there, measured by the ton, indicates that Egyptians were not just harvesting feral or wild populations but, for the first time in history, were actively breeding domestic cats.

Egypt officially prohibited the export of its venerated cats for centuries. Nevertheless, by 2,500 years ago the animals had made their way to Greece, proving the inefficacy of export bans. By 2,000 years ago grain ships sailed directly from Alexandria to destinations throughout the Roman Empire, and cats are certain to have been onboard to keep the rats in check. Thus introduced, cats would have established colonies in port cities and then fanned out from there. Later, when the Romans expanded their empire, domestic cats traveled with them and became common throughout Europe. Evidence for their spread comes from the German site of Tofting in Schleswig, which dates to between the fourth and 10th centuries, as well as increasing references to cats in art and literature from that period. (Oddly, domestic cats seem to have reached the British Isles before the Romans brought them over—a dispersal that researchers cannot yet explain.)

Meanwhile, on the opposite side of the globe, domestic cats had presumably spread to the Orient almost 2,000 years ago, along well-established trade routes between Greece and Rome and the Far East, reaching China by way of Mesopotamia and arriving in India via land and sea. Then something interesting happened. Because no native wildcats with which the newcomers could interbreed lived in the Far East, the Oriental domestic cats soon began evolving along their own trajectory. Small, isolated groups of Oriental domestics gradually acquired distinctive coat colors and other mutations through a process known as genetic drift, in which traits that are neither beneficial nor maladaptive become fixed in a population.

This drift led to the emergence of the Korat, the Siamese, the Birman and other "natural breeds," which were described by Thai Buddhist monks in a book called the *Tamara Maew* (meaning "Cat-Book Poems") that may date back to 1350. The putative antiquity of these breeds received support from the results of genetic studies announced in 2008, in which Marilyn Menotti-Raymond of the National Cancer Institute and Leslie Lyons, now at the University of Missouri, found DNA differences between today's European and Oriental domestic cat breeds indicative of more than 700 years of independent cat breeding in Asia and Europe.

As to when domestic cats reached the Americas, little is known. Christopher Columbus and other seafarers of his day reportedly carried cats with them on transatlantic voyages. And voyagers onboard the *Mayflower* and residents of Jamestown are said to have brought cats with them to control vermin and to bring good luck. How house cats got to Australia is even murkier, although recent DNA analysis by our team affirms that the Australian cats are of a European type (rather than Oriental) and likely arrived with European explorers in the 1600s, 40,000 years after the Aboriginal Australians settled the continent.

Breeding for Beauty

Although humans might have played some minor role in the development of the natural breeds in the Orient, concerted efforts to produce novel breeds did not begin until relatively recently. Even the Egyptians, who we know were breeding cats extensively, do not seem to have been selecting for visible traits, probably because distinctive variants had not yet arisen: in their paintings, both wildcats and house cats are depicted as having the same mackerel-tabby coat. Experts believe that most of the modern breeds were developed in the British Isles in the 19th century, based on the writings of English natural history artist Harrison Weir. And in 1871 the first proper fancy cat breeds—breeds created by humans to achieve a particular appearance—were displayed at a cat show held at the Crystal Palace in London (a Persian won, although the Siamese was a sensation).

Today the Cat Fancier's Association and the International Cat Association recognize nearly 60 breeds of domestic cat. Just a dozen or so genes account for the differences in coat color, fur length and texture, as well as other, subtler coat characteristics, such as shading and shimmer, among these breeds.

Thanks to the sequencing of the entire genome of an Abyssinian cat named Cinnamon in 2007, geneticists have identified the mutations that produce such traits as tabby patterning, black, white and orange coloring, long hair and many others. Beyond differences in the pelage-related genes, however, the genetic variation between domestic cat breeds is very slight—comparable to that seen between adjacent human populations, such as the French and the Italians.

The wide range of sizes, shapes and temperaments that is observed in dogs—consider the Chihuahua and the Great Dane—is absent in cats. Felines show much less variety because, unlike dogs—which were bred from prehistoric times for such tasks as guarding, hunting and herding—early cats were under no such selective breeding pressures. To enter our homes, they had only to evolve a people-friendly disposition.

So are today's house cats truly domesticated? Well, yes, certainly they are—but perhaps only just. Although they satisfy the criterion of tolerating people, most domestic cats are feral and do not rely on people to feed them or to find them mates. And whereas other domesticates, like dogs, look quite distinct from their wild ancestors, the average domestic cat largely retains the wild body plan. It does exhibit a few morphological differences, however—namely slightly shorter legs, a smaller brain and, as Charles Darwin noted, a longer intestine, which may have been an adaptation to scavenging kitchen scraps.

The house cat has not stopped evolving, though—far from it. Armed with artificial insemination and in vitro fertilization technology, cat breeders today are pushing domestic cat genetics into uncharted territory: they are hybridizing house cats with other felid species to create exotic new breeds. The Bengal and the Caracat, for example, resulted from crossing the house cat with the Asian leopard cat and the caracal, respectively. The domestic cat may thus be on the verge of an unprecedented and radical evolution into a multispecies composite whose future can only be imagined.

Referenced

The Natural History of the Wild Cats. Andrew Kitchener. Cornell University Press, Comstock Publishing Associates, 1997.

A Natural History of Domesticated Mammals. Second edition. Juliet Clutton-Brock. Cambridge University Press, Natural History Museum, 1999.

The Near Eastern Origin of Cat Domestication. Carlos A. Driscoll et al. in *Science*, Vol. 317, pages 519–523; 2007.

Patterns of Molecular Genetic Variation among Cat Breeds. Marilyn Menotti-Raymond et al. in *Genomics*, Vol. 91, No. 1, pages 1–11; 2008.

The British Museum Book of Cats. Juliet Clutton-Brock. British Museum Press, Natural History Museum, 2012.

About the Author

Carlos A. Driscoll is at the National Institute on Alcohol Abuse and Alcoholism where he is focused on detecting the causative genes behind domestic behavior. In 2007 he published the first DNA-based family tree of Felis silvestris, the species to which the domestic cat belongs.

Untangling the Mystery of How Fido Became Humankind's Best Friend

By Jason G. Goldman

For decades scientists have debated how, where and when the wolf became the dog. Now a new study hints that dogs were domesticated just once, challenging a previous claim about how many times humans befriended canines.

In a paper published this week in *Nature Communications* Krishna Veeramah at Stony Brook University and colleagues argue that dog domestication occurred once, sometime between 20,000 and 40,000 years ago.

Early efforts at nailing down the time and place of domestication varied wildly. One set of analyses published in the late 1990s suggested dogs and wolves diverged some 135,000 years ago in the Middle East. A 2009 paper placed the divergence much more recently, at 16,300 years ago in southern China. Others have located the series of events that led to canine domestication in Europe, rather than the Middle East or Asia.

Whereas methodological concerns plagued those early studies, modern genomic techniques combined with the ability to extract DNA from well-preserved fossils are inching scientists ever closer to the elusive question of Fido's origins.

At first glance, the findings should not seem all that controversial. Veeramah's timing is well within contemporary estimates. But last year a study published in *Science* made the argument that dog domestication actually occurred twice: once in Europe and once in Asia.

It all comes down to doggy demography.

In his 2016 study Greger Larson, a biologist at the University of Oxford, compared the genomes of modern dogs from across Eurasia with the genome of an ancient dog whose remains were unearthed at an Irish archaeological site, and estimated that Western and

Eastern dog populations diverged between 6,400 and 14,000 years ago, during the Neolithic period. That is later than the earliest archaeological evidence for dogs in both places, which means modern dogs share an ancestor that may in fact be younger than the dogs that had already inhabited both Europe and the Far East during the earlier Stone Age period, the Paleolithic.

Larson takes the findings to suggest that some European wolf gave rise to west Eurasian domestic dogs whereas some Asian wolf gave rise to east Asian domestic dogs. At some point, one of those lineages died out and the other expanded. Based on an analysis of mitochondrial DNA, a collection of genetic material that propagates from mothers to their offspring within each cell's mitochondria, Larson argued it was the European dog population that was replaced as Asian dogs migrated west with their human masters.

Veeramah is quick to point out Larson's analysis hinged largely on the genome of one ancient pooch, extracted from a 5,000-year-old fossilized ear bone preserved at a Neolithic site in Ireland called Newgrange. The current study utilizes that genome as well as two others extracted from fossils uncovered from Neolithic sites in southern Germany—a canine cranium dated to 5,000 years and a skull fragment from an older site, dated to approximately 7,000 years.

By including additional samples of ancient origin as well as ones from a diverse set of modern dogs from around the world, Veeramah's team was able to more finely hone the domestication story. Indeed, the researchers found evidence for genetic continuity in European dogs, rather than replacement by Asian ones, for at least 7,000 years. "We have a 7,000-year-old sample that was nearly indistinguishable from modern domesticated dogs," says University of Michigan biologist Amanda Pendleton, a co-author on the study. Genetically, "it looks just like the dog chewing your left shoe in the closet."

But Larson contends the new paper is generally in agreement with his. "It provides [evidence for] exactly what we did, in terms of the split between East and West," he says, and the two papers place the dog–wolf divergence at around the same time as well. The key trend, for Larson, is taken from the archaeological record. "You get very old dogs on both sides of the Old World but young dogs in the middle," he says. To know whether his hypothesis of dual domestication events is ultimately correct would require uncovering Paleolithic dog fossils from Europe to see how similar—or different— they are from the younger Neolithic ones. If his hypothesis is right, the oldest dogs in western Europe would look very different from their Neolithic counterparts.

Veeramah says the baseline assumption should be a single domestication process in a single place, although he is wary about saying exactly where that might have occurred. "The burden of proof is higher" to support a scenario in which multiple domesticated dog lineages emerged independently in different parts of the planet, he says.

Part of the trouble with accurately charting the evolutionary history of domestic dogs is that animal carcasses do not fossilize very well in some climates (like the tropics), which skews the archaeological record toward those places that do reliably turn up high-quality fossils. And not all ancient human cultures took equal care to preserve the remains of their dogs, even in places where fossilization is a possibility. Moreover, it is not enough for a bone to fossilize; it has to become preserved in such a way that DNA remains extractable. So although there are Paleolithic fossils as old as 30,000 years, finding one with usable DNA fragments is a separate matter entirely.

For the moment, the precise nature of Fido's family tree remains somewhat shrouded in mystery. As more and more fossils are found and their DNA is sequenced, however, the origins of domestic dogs will inevitably become clearer. And then we'll be able to say with greater certainty just how that dog chewing your left shoe in the closet became your best friend.

About the Author

Jason G. Goldman is a science journalist based in Los Angeles. He has written about animal behavior, wildlife biology, conservation, and ecology for Scientific American, Los Angeles *magazine, the* Washington Post, *the* Guardian, *the BBC,*

Conservation magazine, and elsewhere. He contributes to Scientific American's "60-Second Science" podcast, and is co-editor of Science Blogging: The Essential Guide *(Yale University Press). He enjoys sharing his wildlife knowledge on television and on the radio, and often speaks to the public about wildlife and science communication.*

What a Dog Geneticist Wants You to Know about Dog Genetics

D og lovers talk a big game when it comes to genetics. Who hasn't heard someone claim to know which breeds reside within a beloved mutt simply by appearance? And who hasn't heard claims about a dog's underlying "nature" even though geneticists acknowledge nature and nurture work together? DNA is undeniably instrumental to all living beings, but casual beliefs about genetics— particularly dog genetics—aren't always on point.

Not being a geneticist myself and wanting to know what dog lovers tend to get right and wrong about dog genetics, I reached out to an actual geneticist! After completing her PhD in genomics, Jessica Perry Hekman joined the Karlsson Lab at The Broad Institute of MIT and Harvard as a post-doctoral associate. You may be familiar with their citizen science project, *Darwin's Dogs*, which is sequencing dog DNA for free. It's quite an undertaking that's dependent on grant funding, and they have a particular interest in dog behavioral genetics and its applications for dogs and people. In addition to working as a researcher, Hekman has created widely available online webinars and classes relating to genetics, and she also maintains the thoughtful and informative blog, The Dog Zombie.

Here's what Hekman, the dog geneticist, wishes dog lovers knew about genetics:

Q: What do dog lovers seem to get wrong about dog genetics?
A: "Thinking that genetics are destiny—that if a problem is 'genetic,' it can't be changed. Sometimes that's true, but very rarely in the case of behavior problems. A dog's personality is inextricably made up both of genetics and experience, and if you're seeing problem behaviors, it's always worth exploring what it might take to fix them. (On the other hand, if you're trying to get

your retriever to be less interested in balls, this is likely to be an uphill battle.)"

Q: What do you wish purebred dog owners knew about dog genetics?

A: "Inbreeding is real and is a serious problem in many, if not most, pure breeds."

[Hekman has previously weighed in on this topic. In the post 'How to Make the World Better for Dogs' at *Companion Animal Psychology*, Hekman describes a number of well-known challenges that purebred dogs face. Here's Hekman: "We can make the world better for dogs by making dogs who fit into the world better. I would love to see dog owners draw a line in the sand and insist on dogs with muzzles long enough to let them breathe normally, or dogs who are not born with a 60% chance of developing cancer at some point in their lives due to their breed, or dogs whose heads are too big for them to be born without a C-section. I'd love to see more breeders taking matters into their own hands and starting to experiment with how we breed dogs instead of continuing to use dogs from within breeds lacking in genetic diversity. I'd love to see more breed clubs supporting outcrossing projects to bring an influx of genetic diversity and healthy alleles into their breed. I'd love more dog lovers to become aware of the problems with how we breed dogs—how even the most responsible breeders breed dogs! This year, it is time for change."]

Q: What do you wish mixed-breed dog owners knew about dog genetics?

A: "Finding out the breeds that make up your mixed breed dog is unlikely to be helpful in predicting your dog's behavior or future health problems. It's just fun!"

[Speaking of mutts, MuttMix is a new, online, citizen science survey by *Darwin's Dogs* and the International Association of Animal Behavior Consultants (IAABC) exploring if people can visually identify the predominant breed in mutts. Based on earlier studies, this might be more difficult than you'd think. Give it a try!]

In the study of heritability (particularly regarding dog behavior traits) is there an area that has the most potential for advancing the field? "Sample size! This is why I am throwing my lot in with *Darwin's Dogs*. Elinor Karlsson, the head of the project, firmly believes that the way to crack the problem of 'which genes affect behavior' is to look at lots and lots and lots of dogs. She has me convinced. We have succeeded in building a base of people who have given us access to their dogs' DNA and answered so many questions about their dogs, for which we are extremely grateful. Now we just need the funding to sequence all those dogs!"

The views expressed are those of the author(s) and are not necessarily those of Scientific American.

About the Author

Julie Hecht is a Ph.D. student studying dog behavior and writes the Dog Spies blog at ScientificAmerican.com.

Good News for Dogs with Cancer

By Amy Sutherland

Truman's owners first thought he had twisted his ankle: The Bernese mountain dog was limping and might have landed awkwardly after jumping off the couch. But when he was still hobbled a few days later, they got an x-ray. The scan revealed that Truman had osteosarcoma, a deadly, fast-moving bone cancer that typically strikes breeds of large dogs. The owners' veterinarian told them amputating Truman's leg, followed by chemotherapy, might buy them another year or so with their fun-loving clown. They opted for the surgery and took one important extra step: enrolling him in a clinical trial at Tufts University that was studying an experimental vaccine for osteosarcoma. Nearly two years since his diagnosis, Truman remains cancer-free. He gets along fine with three legs and turned nine early this month, which he celebrated with a car ride and dog-friendly carrot cake.

Life, at long last, is improving for dogs with cancer, the number-one killer of beloved pets. An estimated one in three dogs get the disease. Some pure breeds, such as golden retrievers and boxers, are especially prone to it. Yet for decades, there was scant research into canine cancer, and consequently, veterinarians had little to offer sick pets and their distraught owners.

That situation has begun to change since researchers realized that dogs might be able to solve some of the mysteries of human cancer. Several scientists believe pet dogs are better research models than lab mice for this disease, as well as some other illnesses. Our dogs share our lives, drinking the same water and breathing the same air. Their diseases occur naturally like ours, as opposed to being introduced artificially in lab mice. We also have more in common with dogs biologically than we do with mice, and cancer is often caused by the same genetic mutations in both species.

Those factors are why clinical trials using pet dogs have increased over the past decades, especially in oncology. These tests examine new therapies for canine cancer that might inform research in human cancer treatment. The National Cancer Institute, an arm of the U.S. National Institutes of Health, has been a major supporter of this new work. In 2017 the NCI gave out $11.5 million in grants to six veterinary schools to study immunotherapy treatments for four different cancers in pet dogs. NCI funding, plus more from pharmacological companies, has made for boom times in canine cancer research. "Dogs are helping us understand a very complex puzzle," says Amy LeBlanc, a veterinary oncologist who directs the Comparative Oncology Program at the NCI. "Not only do we have more research, but the sophistication of that research has exploded."

Though the overarching goal of these comparative trials is to help humans, they have produced a number of promising cancer drugs for dogs. In 2017 the U.S. Food and Drug Administration conditionally approved Tanovea-CA1 to fight canine lymphoma. And an osteosarcoma vaccine under development by Aratana Therapeutics has been conditionally approved by the U.S. Department of Agriculture. Other drugs are well along in the clinical study pipeline, such as verdinexor for treating lymphoma in dogs.

New treatment techniques and diagnostic tools have likewise been created. Technology for targeted radiation that avoids damaging tissue near a tumor was developed on pet dogs with sinus tumors at the University of Wisconsin–Madison. Now the next generation of that therapy, Radixact, works on a wider range of tumors, even ones that move, such as in lung cancer, says David Vail, a professor of veterinary oncology who designs comparative clinical trials at the university. And a new liquid biopsy has made canine bladder cancer, which can be mistaken for bladder stones or urinary tract infections, easy to diagnose, even in an early stage. Developed by a team at North Carolina State University, the technique screens for the tell-tale signs of cancer in a urine test.

Genetic research into canine cancer, which has lagged far behind the human version, has gotten a boost as well. The DNA of canine osteosarcoma cells was sequenced this past summer by researchers at Tufts. The NCI has given money to sequence DNA for at least five other canine cancers, including melanoma, B-cell lymphoma and bladder cancer. Cheryl London, a veterinary oncologist at Tufts and an expert in comparative oncology, predicts that the next five years will see an explosion of genetic information, and that will lead to more effective and less toxic treatments for dogs with cancer.

These clinical trials have also given owners with dangerously sick dogs somewhere to turn. The osteosarcoma vaccine study that helped Truman was run by the NCI at 11 universities. Not only do these trials provide experimental medicine that may save a dog's life, most do it at a price any dog owner can afford: free. "We now have access to some of the latest and greatest cutting-edge medicine for dogs," says Nicole Ehrhart, a veterinarian at Colorado State University who helped pioneer limb-salvaging techniques for dogs with bone cancer.

The boom in canine cancer research has inspired some scientists to think very big. This past spring, the largest veterinary clinical study in history began to test a vaccine meant to stop any type of cancer before it becomes a tumor. By its conclusion, 800 dogs will have been injected with the boosters or a placebo and tracked for five years. And Ehrhart, who also directs Colorado State University's Columbine Health Systems Center for Healthy Aging, is devising studies with pet dogs to better understand old age, which she calls the root problem of cancer. "This it where it gets exciting and futuristic," Ehrhart says. "If we could slow down aging, we would make such impact on these diseases."

People would also have their pets longer—the dream of anyone with a dog curled up at their feet, especially a sick one. "What people forget about veterinary medicine," London says, "is that I'm also treating the person on the other end of the leash."

About the Author

Amy Sutherland is a journalist and author who writes about animal and human behavior.

What Is a Dog Anyway?

By Pat Shipman

The geographer Jared Diamond has called domestication the worst mistake humans ever made. He blames domestication for the rise of monoculture, which he says leads to a larger, more sedentary human population in which disease can spread rapidly. On top of that, settled populations dependent upon crops become more vulnerable to climate change, plant diseases and natural disasters. Domestication, Diamond says, also caused a precipitous decline in biodiversity, and a rise in social inequality and warfare among humans.

Sounds like a pretty bad choice.

And yet, the first domestication—the turning of wolves into dogs—was an impressive feat. Humans at the time had to evaluate each new species they encountered: Will it kill me, or can I kill it? If it kills me, how is it stronger or more skillful than I? If I kill it, what can I gain?

Eventually, humans began to appreciate that not killing, but living with, another species could be useful. Paradoxically, our ancestors chose one of the most dangerous predators they knew to try to live with: the gray wolf. I'm a paleoanthropologist who has been researching the effects of domestication. The origin of dogs is contentious, but I hypothesize that domesticating wolves into dogs may have helped the first modern humans to outcompete other hominins like Neandertals.

What was the advantage of cooperating with wolves? Modern wolves have greater endurance than humans and a top speed of up to 40 miles per hour, versus 30 to 45 mph in dogs and only 27 mph in a world-class runner like Usain Bolt. Compared with humans, wolves have a superior sense of smell (they have more than 50 times the smell receptors), sharper teeth and claws, and better night vision. Borrowing or co-opting these abilities provided a substantial improvement in humans' hunting and survival. But the wild wolf had to benefit from the arrangement. The main advantage to the canids would have been that their role was to find the prey, track it and surround it while humans with distance weapons did the dangerous job of bringing a prey animal down and killing it. In independent studies, Karen Lupo and Jeremy Koster have shown that hunting with a dog yields more meat per hour of effort than hunting without one, despite the fact that the dogs eat some of the meat.

Domestication is not taming, like that used with wild-born Asian elephants, which must be laboriously trained anew with each generation. In fact, most animals that humans have attempted to domesticate have refused. A striking example is the beautiful zebra, which, though closely related to the domestic horse and donkey, remains one of most dangerous animals in the zoo.

Because domestication of any animal involves selection (by humans) for genetic traits, it takes generations to accomplish. Some scholars see the earliest changes about 30,000 years ago, while others see domesticated dogs only by about 16,000 years ago. Remarkably, humans tried to domesticate not only the gentle or tasty animals, like cows and sheep, but also fierce competitors vying with us for food, water and safe places to raise their young. I hypothesize that allying with wolves allowed modern *Homo sapiens* to outcompete and out-survive earlier species like Neandertals who had lived successfully in Europe long before modern humans got there. I see no startlingly large change in weapons in the earliest modern human sites that would account for their survival. Dogs would have helped modern humans not only in hunting but also in guarding the carcass from scavengers after the kill.

Dogs excel at an unusually broad set of tasks: acting as companions; as haulers of loads; as guardians and living weapons; as detectors of disease or contraband; and as trackers. They provide fur, meat, potentially useful bones for making tools, and more dogs. They are especially good at being living blankets. Dog bones or teeth have also served as jewelry, identifying members in a particular human group. Despite the inherent risks of associating closely with another large carnivore, this versatility may have spurred the proliferation of dog breeds in the 18th and 19th centuries. In fact, one's job or social status has long been signaled by the dog one owns, from the Pekingese of Chinese royalty to the saluki, the racing dog of Egyptian kings, the corgis of the late Queen Elizabeth II, and the sheep-guarding great Pyrenees.

So, why is the origin of dogs contentious? We don't know how to define what a dog is. First, there is no single trait that we can observe in modern or ancient canids that marks them as dogs. Dogs have a look about them and familiar behavior, but no single definitive trait. Genetically, the number of genes that makes a dog a dog is hard to quantify, even if we have the whole genome of a specimen. For example, in maternally inherited mitochondrial DNA, there are about 16,000 base pairs. How many genes must be sequenced to identify a species? We don't know because there are mutations that occur but don't have much effect. How many must be changed to make the specimen no longer a wolf but a dog? Basically, we don't know.

Second, there is a fundamental problem with dating the progression of wolf to dog. If the specimen is less than 50,000 years old, bones, charcoal and other organic substances can be dated based on the percentage of radioactive carbon that has degraded to a nonradioactive nitrogen. Geneticists use the number of mutations in the genome to date specimens, but mutations may occur faster or slower than "normal." Genetic dating is not precise. Importantly, not all animals get preserved as fossils, so much of the record of life on earth is invisible.

Finally, I fear we have neglected part of the evidence—where the iconic Australian dingo fits in. After evolving in Africa, modern humans reached Australia before they reached Central Europe, the Americas or Antarctica. Madjedbebe, the earliest archaeological site in Australia, is dated to about 65,000 years ago. Researchers who accept this date can find no trace of dogs or any domestic canids anywhere in the world at this time. Genetic estimates suggest that dingoes got to Australia up to about 18,000 years ago, but there are no dingo bones earlier than about 4,000 years ago. Could they have been in Australia so long and left no traces?

Dingoes figure prominently in the Indigenous culture and mythology of Australians, but dingoes or their ancestors are not marsupials, like every other large-bodied mammal endemic to Australia. (Every placental mammal in Australia—true dogs, horses, rabbits, cats and rats, for example—has been brought in by people.) Sadly, many researchers investigating the origin of dogs have discounted dingoes as unimportant, but they are the only alternative story of the transformation of wild canids into dogs that we have. Dingoes' distinctive traits are fascinating. Why do they climb and manipulate objects with their paws so well? Why do they howl but not bark? Why do they reproduce only once a year like wolves and mature slowly? Why are they so resistant to being in captivity? What makes dingoes different from dogs? Was it how the Indigenous people of Australia lived, leading to a different sort of domestication, as Adam Brumm and Loukas Koungoulus have suggested? Was it the isolation from other canids? Did dingo ancestors have something lacking in later canids?

We take for granted the origins of this species we hold so dear. But to really understand what a dog is, we need to ask more questions.

This is an opinion and analysis article, and the views expressed by the author or authors are not necessarily those of Scientific American.

About the Author

Pat Shipman has an M.A. and Ph.D. in biological anthropology from New York University and is interested in how humans and their ancestors fit into their ecosystems. She has written more than 150 articles in popular science magazines and professional journals, in addition to three biographies and eleven science books.

Section 2: Exploring How Animals Communicate

Wolves Have Local Howl Accents

By Jason G. Goldman

S he has this thing where she goes to a movie theater, watching a horror movie and there was a wolf howling in the background." University of Cambridge zoologist Arik Kershenbaum, talking about his collaborator Holly Root-Gutteridge, a biologist at Syracuse University. "She said to herself, 'Well, that's wrong. That's clearly a European wolf and not a North American wolf like it should be in the scene.'"

Slight variations in the way we speak allow us to tell whether someone is from Boston or New York just by listening to them. The same turns out to be true for the animals known as canids, which includes wolves, dogs and coyotes. They all howl to communicate—but those howls vary. Canids can tell which howls belong to their known associates and which belong to strangers.

So Kershenbaum and Root-Gutteridge decided to categorize the howls of different canids around the world. Together with colleagues, they compiled recordings of more than 2,000 canid howls, including European wolves, Mexican wolves, arctic wolves, dingoes, coyotes, golden jackals, domestic dogs, New Guinea singing dogs, and more. A computer program sorted the howls into different types. The study was published in the journal *Behavioral Processes*. [Arik Kershenbaum et al, Disentangling canid howls across multiple species and subspecies: Structure in a complex communication channel]

Based on the analysis, canids use 21 different kinds of howls to communicate. If you think of the howls as words, then all canids have the same vocabulary—but each species or sub-species has its own unique dialect. Some words are more common in one dialect, while other words are more common in another dialect and so on. By matching dialect with species and geography, researchers could monitor endangered species, like red wolves, just by listening.

[AK:] "Being able to distinguish between the howls of a coyote and the howls of a red wolf opens the possibility for techniques

40

of passive monitoring, passive population monitoring, using acoustics."

Meanwhile, ranchers have tried to broadcast specific howls to discourage grey wolves from feasting on their livestock, but it's never been successful.

[AK:] "Because we don't really know what message we're conveying to the wolves when we play back an arbitrary howl. For all we know, we could be playing back a howl that means come and eat, there's lots of interesting food over here."

The research could thus finally bring peace to the conflict between ranchers and wolves, by finally speaking to the predators in their own language.

—Jason G. Goldman

[The above text is a transcript of this podcast.]

About the Author

Jason G. Goldman is a science journalist based in Los Angeles. He has written about animal behavior, wildlife biology, conservation, and ecology for Scientific American, Los Angeles *magazine, the* Washington Post, *the* Guardian, *the* BBC, Conservation *magazine, and elsewhere. He contributes to* Scientific American's *"60-Second Science" podcast, and is co-editor of* Science Blogging: The Essential Guide *(Yale University Press). He enjoys sharing his wildlife knowledge on television and on the radio, and often speaks to the public about wildlife and science communication.*

How Do Bonobos and Chimpanzees Talk to One Another?

By Felicity Muth

For the next few articles, I will be featuring interviews with female researchers in animal behaviour (from students to assistant professors), talking about a recent discovery they made. This week's interview is with Kirsty Graham.

Kirsty Graham is a PhD student at the University of St Andrews, Scotland, who works on gestural communication of chimpanzees and bonobos in Uganda and DRCongo. I recently asked her some questions about the work that she does and some exciting recent findings of hers about how these animals communicate.

Q: How did you become interested in communication, and specifically gestures?

A: Languages are fascinating–the diversity, the culture, the learning–and during undergrad, I became interested in the origins of our language ability. I went to Quest University Canada (a small liberal arts university) and learned that I could combine my love of languages and animals and being outdoors! Other great apes don't have language in the way that humans do, but studying different aspects of communication, such as gestures, may reveal how language evolved. Although my interest really started from an interest in languages, once you get so deep into studying other species you become excited about their behaviour for its own sake. In the long run, it would be nice to piece together how language evolved, but for now I'm starting with a very small piece of the puzzle–bonobo gestures.

Q: How do you study gestures in non-human primates?

A: There are a few different approaches to studying gestures: in the wild or in captivity; through observation or with experiments;

studying one gesture in detail or looking at the whole repertoire. I chose to observe wild bonobos and look at their whole repertoire. Since not much is known about bonobo gestural communication, this seemed like a good starting point. During my PhD, I spent 12 months at Wamba (Kyoto University's research site) in the DRCongo. I filmed the bonobos, anticipating the beginning of social interactions so that I could record the gestures that they use. Then I spent a long time watching the videos, finding gestures, and coding information about the gestures.

Q: What's it like working out in the field with chimps and bonobos?

A: Fieldwork is great! It can be pretty lonely sometimes and physically exhausting, but field observation is imperative for figuring out a species' natural behaviour. Fieldwork and captive experiments complement one another. At Wamba, the bonobos are very well habituated, so we can observe them at a distance of 5-10m when they're on the ground. I'm now at Kalinzu doing a pilot study on chimpanzees. Sometimes you have excellent days, where the apes are all travelling together, and sit and groom on a log in a clearing while all the infants are playing. Those are great data days. But sometimes you have a day where it rains and the apes spend all morning in their nests! It's a mixed bag, but overall it's a pretty fun job.

Q: I think I know what gestures are from when I communicate with people, but how can you decide what counts as a gesture for a non-human animal?

A: A gesture is a body movement (arms, legs, head, torso) that is performed intentionally in order to communicate something to another individual. Bonobos raise their arms, flap their legs, shake their heads, thrust their hips, just to name a few gestures. There are silent-visual gestures like waving, audible gestures like clapping, and contact gestures like slapping someone on the back. A gesture should be directed towards another individual (no random arm flailing while sitting on your own); the signaller should check that the recipient is paying attention (what's the point in waving at you if you're facing the other way?) and select an appropriate gesture (e.g. a tap on the shoulder if the recipient is looking away); and if the recipient doesn't respond to the gesture, the signaller should persist or elaborate. These criteria show that the signaller has a goal in mind, something that they want to communicate, and are using gestures to achieve that goal.

Chimpanzees use around seventy gesture types in the wild, and they produce gestures intentionally, aiming to affect the behaviour of the recipient. Chimpanzee gestures are used to request a variety of behaviour, from begging for food to requesting sex. But chimpanzees are not our *only* closest living relative–the bonobo is equally related to humans. Comparing the two species offers insight into how gesture evolved. My research so far has focused on the bonobo, trying to fill in this gap in our knowledge.

We found that the bonobos at Wamba have a vocabulary of 68 gesture types. The overlap with published data for chimpanzees (at Budongo research site in Uganda) was roughly 90%. Such a large overlap points toward a genetically channelled repertoire of gestures–if the gestures were all individually learned, we would expect more differences between species and even between populations and individuals. The chimpanzee repertoire overlaps around 80% with orangutans and 60% with gorillas, and so it is likely that our last common ancestor used many of these gestures.

Our study was the first to look at each individual's "understood repertoire," which is similar to what linguists would call a "receptive vocabulary"–the words that a person can understand, whether or not they ever use them. One can measure the "expressed repertoire" by seeing what gestures an individual deploys, but for the "understood repertoire," one must see what gesture types the individual receives and responds to in a way that satisfies the signaller. This is also how I figure out what a gesture means–if Bonobo A does an "arm raise" gesture *and* Bonobo B responds by starting to groom the signaller, and Bonobo A seems satisfied with that response (i.e. they don't keep gesturing), then the meaning of "arm raise" in this instance was "please groom me." In that case, "arm raise" would be in Bonobo A's expressed repertoire and Bonobo B's understood repertoire.

When we grouped bonobos by age or by sex, then each group had most gestures in their expressed and understood repertoire. For example, both males and females can both express and understand the gesture "Reach." In fact, of the 47 gesture types that were seen more than three times, forty-two were both used and expressed by males and females, young and adult. Specific gestures are not being produced only by males and received only by females, or only by young and only by old, rather this is a mutually understood communication system in which all individuals have the potential to be both signaller and recipient for almost all gesture types.

Language is also a communication system where any native speaker can have access to the same words as any other native speaker. This mutual understanding of signals is required to communicate about goals that anyone might want and anyone might give. For bonobos and chimpanzees, these activities include play, grooming, feeding, travelling together, and sex. At some point, it became necessary for our human ancestors to communicate about more than these immediate goals, and therein lies the mystery of language evolution.

Q: How similar are the chimpanzee and bonobo gestures to our own? What can your findings tell us about the evolution of human gestures?

A: Good question! We don't know exactly how many gestures humans share with chimpanzees and bonobos because we learn a lot of gestures alongside language. By the time infants are old enough to start using gestures, they are also learning words and conventional gestures of the culture that they're growing up in. Observation of humans is therefore inadequate for seeing which gestures are shared with other apes. Byrne and Cochet wrote a neat paper, "Where have all the (ape) gestures gone?," suggesting an experiment to test whether naïve human observers could understand other apes' gestures.

Our findings tell us that given the overlap of all great ape gestures, early humans likely also shared this gestural repertoire. Gestures are an important way for great apes to communicate, they use them to request food, grooming, and sex. But there are other aspects to communication as well, such as vocalisations and facial expressions. New research that looks at how great ape communication works across all of these modalities is necessary before we can start to answer the difficult questions of how language evolved. If these other forms of communication are sufficient for other species of great apes, then why language?

Referenced

Graham, K.E., Furuichi, T. & Byrne, R.W. (2016) The gestural repertoire of the wild bonobo (*Pan paniscus*): a mutually understood communication system. *Animal Cognition* doi:10.1007/s10071-016-1035-9

The views expressed are those of the author(s) and are not necessarily those of Scientific American.

About the Author

Felicity Muth is an early-career researcher with a PhD in animal cognition.

The First "Google Translate" for Elephants Debuts

By Rachel Nuwer

When a male African savanna elephant folds his ears while simultaneously waving them, he's ready for a fight. When a female folds her ears and accompanies the action with an ear flap, that means she's also issuing a serious threat. But when elephants come together and fold their ears while also rapidly flapping them, the animals are expressing a warm, affiliative greeting that is part of their bonding ceremonies.

Elephants possess an incredibly rich repertoire of communication techniques, including hundreds of calls and gestures that convey specific meanings and can change depending on the context. Different elephant populations also exhibit culturally learned behaviors unique to their specific group. Elephant behaviors are so complex, in fact, that even scientists may struggle to keep up with them all. Now, to get the animals and researchers on the same page, a renowned biologist who has been studying endangered savanna elephants for nearly 50 years has co-developed a digital elephant ethogram, a repository of everything known about their behavior and communication.

"Without a multimedia approach, I see it as impossible to properly show and explain the behavior of a species, and we hope this will inspire other scientists to take a similar approach for other species," says Joyce Poole, co-founder and scientific director of ElephantVoices, a nonprofit science and conservation organization, and co-creator of the new ethogram. "At a time when biodiversity is plummeting and the lives of elephants are being heavily impacted by humans, we also want to spell out to the world what we stand to lose."

Poole built the easily searchable public database with her husband and research partner Petter Granli after they came to realize that scientific papers alone would no longer cut it for cataloging the discoveries they and others were making. The Elephant Ethogram currently includes more than 500 behaviors depicted through nearly 3,000 annotated videos, photographs and audio files. The entries encompass the majority, if not all, of typical elephant behaviors, which Poole and Granli gleaned from more than 100 references spanning more than 100 years, with the oldest records dating back to 1907. About half of the described behaviors came from the two investigators' own studies and observations, while the rest came from around seven other leading savanna elephant research teams.

While the ethogram is primarily driven by Poole and Granli's observations, "there are very few, if any, examples of behaviors described in the literature that we have not seen ourselves," Poole points out. The project is also just beginning, she adds, because it is meant to be a living catalog that scientists actively contribute to as new findings come in.

"We know elephants behave and communicate with each other in complex ways. But until now, we have barely scratched the surface of just how complex that behavior and communication is," says Lucy Bates, a visiting research fellow specializing in elephant cognition at the University of Sussex in England, who was not involved in creating the ethogram. "Now we have this foundation—freely available in the public domain—from which we can build a much more comprehensive picture of what elephants are doing and why."

Ethograms are compilations of animal activities and behaviors, either in a specific context or for a species overall. Researchers use ethograms for studying behavior and making comparisons among ages, sexes, families, populations or different species. While a digital ethogram exists for laboratory mice, and another has been published in written form for chimpanzees, Poole and Granli believe the exhaustive, digitized Elephant Ethogram is the first of its kind for any nonhuman wild animal. The multimedia-based nature of the project is important, Poole adds, because with descriptions based only on the written word, audio files or photographs, "it is hard to show the often subtle differences in movement that differentiate one behavior from another."

When Poole began studying elephants in 1975, scientists knew very little about their behavior. Her early research focused on musth, a periodic reproductive condition in male elephants that is characterized by testosterone surges and heightened aggression. Poole noted that the animals waved their ears as a threat, and she sometimes also noticed a low, pulsating sound accompanying this movement. At first, she thought it was produced by the ears whooshing through the air, but she soon realized that the sound was a vocalization. She began to wonder if the animals were making other sounds too low for her ears to fully detect.

To follow up on these observations, Poole teamed up with acoustic biologist Katy Payne. Together, they revealed that the different rumbles elephants produce contain some frequencies below the level of human hearing and that some of these sounds are so powerful they may be heard by other elephants miles away. This discovery helped solve a number of elephant mysteries, including how members of a family are able to quickly find one another after they split up and how the animals, without seeming to make a sound, are able to act in complete unison when a threat is detected.

"For a long time, people talked about elephant ESP," Poole says. "Some vocalizations they make are so powerful and are transmitted through the ground as vibrations, acting like a kind of bush telegraph for elephants saying, 'There's trouble.'"

As Poole continued to study elephants, she realized that the meaning of many of the behaviors she was documenting also changed depending on the context. Tail swatting, for example, is usually used by one elephant to tell another to back off because it is standing too close. But mothers also use tail swatting to keep tabs on infants standing behind them. In still other contexts, elephants use it to pester or nag for attention.

For now, the majority of entries in the Elephant Ethogram come from three locations: Maasai Mara National Reserve, or the Mara, and Amboseli National Park in Kenya and Gorongosa National Park in Mozambique. The limited number of sites do not necessarily affect the breadth of behaviors in the database, however, because most elephant behaviors are conserved across populations. But the frequency of certain behaviors may differ depending on the study site. Elephants at Amboseli, for example, never dig for minerals because the soil there is salty, and Poole has only once seen an Amboseli elephant shake a tree to knock down seed pods because there are very few trees in the area. In the Mara, on the other hand, elephants often dig for minerals. And in Gorongosa, they frequently shake trees for seeds.

Stark cultural differences can also exist among populations. During the Mozambican Civil War, 90 percent of the elephants in Gorongosa were killed for their ivory and meat. Nearly 30 years later, the elephants there still act fearfully and aggressively toward people. "Their behavior is very different from Amboseli and the Mara, where we see almost no defensive behaviors toward people," Poole says. "As Gorongosa experiences a rebirth under new protection and restoration, how long will it take for elephants to abandon those traditions?"

The answer will likely someday be cataloged in the Elephant Ethogram. Now that the project is online, Poole hopes other researchers will begin contributing their own observations and discoveries, broadening the database to include cultural findings from additional savanna elephant populations and unusual behaviors Poole and Granli might have missed. Wildlife photographer Kelly Fogel, for example, recently submitted rare footage of an elephant eating her own placenta after giving birth. And Elephant Aware, a nonprofit conservation group, sent in a similarly uncommon video of a calf trying to suckle from her dead mother. "Now that the Elephant Ethogram is publicly available, we hope that more of our colleagues will share unusual footage from their populations," Poole says.

Already, though, the ethogram is an "invaluable tool" for young scientists who are interested in conducting field research on elephants, says Michael Pardo, a postdoctoral researcher studying African elephant vocal communication at Colorado State University. The ethogram will also help ensure that scientists are talking about the same thing when referring to a specific behavior, he says. "This is really important, because all too often in the scientific literature, confusion about terminology and definitions can result in researchers talking past one another," Pardo adds.

Daniela Hedwig, a research associate at the Elephant Listening Project at Cornell University, agrees that the Elephant Ethogram is "a monumental achievement." Hedwig studies communication in forest elephants in other parts of Africa, and the savanna elephant database will be "an extremely useful repository to draw comparisons between the two species," she says.

Cynthia Moss, director of the Amboseli Trust for Elephants in Kenya, says the ethogram will also be particularly helpful in assessing the lives of captive elephants. Elephants held at circuses, zoos and work environments are deprived of intricate social connections and the ability to travel and to interact with a diverse environment, Poole says. This causes them to suffer from boredom and to develop stereotypic behaviors, such as rocking back and forth. The Elephant Ethogram can shed light on the severity of behavior differences between captive and wild animals, Poole says, and strengthen the case for ending elephant captivity.

Moss adds that the database will also be a valuable tool for wildlife managers and conservationists who seek to differentiate between natural, healthy elephant behaviors and ones induced by stressful conditions, such as poaching and habitat loss. The need for such comparisons is growing as elephants in the wild face mounting pressure to tailor their behaviors to a people-dominated world. "Elephants' ability to culturally adapt is going to be critical for their future survival," Poole says. "As they are forced to change, we're going to learn a lot more about their creativity and flexibility."

About the Author

Rachel Nuwer is a freelance science journalist and author who regularly contributes to Scientific American, *the* New York Times *and* National Geographic, *among other publications. Follow Nuwer on Twitter @RachelNuwer.*

"Chatty Turtles" Flip the Script on the Evolutionary Origins of Vocalization in Animals

By Pakinam Amer

Pakinam Amer: This is *Scientific American*'s 60-Second Science. I'm Pakinam Amer.

Clicks, clucks, grunts and snorts—these are not sounds that we typically associate with turtles.

[CLIP: Audio of South American juvenile turtles]

Amer: They're actually thought to be very quiet or even silent. But it looks like we may have grossly underestimated how much sound they can make. Now a new study in *Nature Communications* has collected vocal recordings from 53 species of turtles and other animals that were otherwise considered to be mute.

[CLIP: Audio of South American juvenile turtles]

Amer: Those clicks you've just heard were calls made by baby giant Amazon River turtles swimming together. A group of evolutionary biologists and other scientists in five different countries pored over these recordings and combined them with vocal repertoires of about 1,800 animal species from other studies.

Amer: They were able to piece together evidence that the last common ancestor of all lungfish and tetrapods started vocalizing more than 400 million years ago. (And just in case you aren't familiar, tetrapods are four-limbed vertebrates that include amphibians, mammals, birds and reptiles.) That's at least 100 million years earlier than previous studies had suggested.

Amer: The new revelations amount to a rewriting of the acoustic history of animals with backbones.

Gabriel Jorgewich-Cohen: I did fieldwork in the Brazilian Amazon with a researcher that published one of these first papers showing that turtles can communicate acoustically, and that inspired me. So I went back home, and I got a piece of equipment, and I started recording my own pets. And I discovered that they were producing sounds as well, and the species I had were not known to produce sounds. So I started thinking maybe they all do, and I went out there, and I recorded as many as I could *[laughs]*.

Amer: That was Gabriel Jorgewich-Cohen, a researcher at the University of Zurich and study co-author. By the way, the pets he's talking about are giant Amazon River turtles, more commonly known as red-eared slider turtles in the U.S.

Jorgewich-Cohen: This is the only species known to have post-hatch parental care among all turtles, which is pretty amazing. And they discovered this by recording the sounds of the animal—not only this species but also sea turtles, for example. When they are in the nest, the hatchlings start vocalizing from within the egg to synchronize hatch. And also when they come out altogether, they individually have less chance of being eaten by another animal. And in the case of the Amazon River turtle, when they go to the water, the females are there, waiting for them, and they are also vocalizing. And they find each other, and then they migrate together up the river to the forest.

Amer: A previous study published in 2020 by researchers at the University of Arizona concluded that only two of 14 families of turtles vocalized. It also stated that acoustic communication evolved independently in most major tetrapod groups, with origins in the range of 100 million to 200 million years ago. But now we know that's not the case.

Jorgewich-Cohen: I was very surprised—happily surprised—when I found so many different types of sounds. And I kept recording more and more animals. And every animal I recorded made sounds; I had no negative results whatsoever. And that was surprising by itself.

Amer: Jorgewich-Cohen recorded hundreds of hours' worth of footage over two years—not just of turtles but also of lungfish, tuatara and other creatures. Animals typically produce sounds for many reasons: to define territory, to attract a mate or to communicate with their young ones. It's a useful skill.

Jorgewich-Cohen: I found that for many turtle species, there are sounds that are only made by males, there are some that are only made by females, and some only by juveniles, and some that males will only make when they are in front of the female.

Amer: If there's one animal from this study that I would've sworn is 100 percent mute, it's the caecilian. For those who're not familiar, let me paint a little picture: Caecilians are slippery, slimy and slithery little things. They burrow, and they look like earthworms or even snakes. But they're neither. They're in fact amphibians. They have a backbone and a skull, jaws and all, but no limbs. And like many tetrapods, they emit sounds through their respiratory tract, just like their common ancestor. It's actually not very easy to come across one.

Jorgewich-Cohen: The caecilian was a special one because I definitely expected it not to make any sounds. And it's not only that it does, but it makes very strange and very loud sounds.

[CLIP: Audio of caecilain]

Amer: Not to be crass, but that sounds a bit like a fart.

Jorgewich-Cohen: When I heard it for the first time, I started laughing, and I sent it to my friends who did fieldwork with me. They also started laughing, and they said, "I cannot believe you. You made the sound with your mouth, and you're sending me the file." I was like, "No, I swear."

Amer: The study, "Common Evolutionary Origin of Acoustic Communication in Choanate Vertebrates," is less focused on the function of these sounds and more on the evolution of acoustic signals. But in future studies, the researchers plan to dig deeper by analyzing the sounds further in an attempt to understand what they mean.

Jorgewich-Cohen: We try to also make footage of the animals while we're recording the sounds so we could try to correlate any type of behavior to the sound that they were making and try to understand how they use the sounds or what ideas they convey.

Amer: Sometimes Jorgewich-Cohen and his colleagues would find more than 30 different sounds in a single species' repertoire. It seems that the more socialized the animal is, the more vocally diverse it is, he says. But further studies are needed to confirm this.

Jorgewich-Cohen: Hopefully this is the beginning of a new field of study. So people are going to go out there and try to record more of these animals and get to new conclusions and new discoveries. But it will be really cool if we could, for example, do playback experiments and try to understand if they reply to the sounds we make. And then we can start understanding what these sounds mean and how they are used.

Amer: Thank you for listening! For *Scientific American*'s 60-Second Science, I'm Pakinam Amer.

[The above text is a transcript of this podcast.]

How Scientists Are Using
AI to Talk to Animals

By Sophie Bushwick

I n the 1970s a young gorilla known as Koko drew worldwide attention with her ability to use human sign language. But skeptics maintain that Koko and other animals that "learned" to speak (including chimpanzees and dolphins) could not truly understand what they were "saying"—and that trying to make other species use human language, in which symbols represent things that may not be physically present, is futile.

"There's one set of researchers that's keen on finding out whether animals can engage in symbolic communication and another set that says, 'That is anthropomorphizing. We need to ... understand nonhuman communication on its own terms,'" says Karen Bakker, a professor at the University of British Columbia and a fellow at the Harvard Radcliffe Institute for Advanced Study. Now scientists are using advanced sensors and artificial intelligence technology to observe and decode how a broad range of species, including plants, already share information with their own communication methods. This field of "digital bioacoustics" is the subject of Bakker's new book *The Sounds of Life: How Digital Technology Is Bringing Us Closer to the Worlds of Animals and Plants.*

Scientific American spoke with Bakker about how technology can help humans communicate with creatures such as bats and honeybees—and how these conversations are forcing us to rethink our relationship with other species.

[An edited transcript of the interview follows.]

Q: Can you give us a brief history of humans attempting to communicate with animals?

A: There were numerous attempts in the mid-20th century to try to teach human language to nonhumans, primates such as Koko.

And those efforts were somewhat controversial. Looking back, one view we have now (that may not have been so prevalent then) is that we were too anthropocentric in our approaches. The desire then was to assess nonhuman intelligence by teaching nonhumans to speak like we do—when in fact we should have been thinking about their abilities to engage in complex communication on their own terms, in their own embodied way, in their own worldview. One of the terms used in the book is the notion of *umwelt*, which is this notion of the lived experience of organisms. If we are attentive to the *umwelt* of another organism, we wouldn't expect a honeybee to speak human language, but we would become very interested in the fascinating language of honeybees, which is vibrational and positional. It's sensitive to nuances such as the polarization of sunlight that we can't even begin to convey with our bodies. And that is where the science is today. The field of digital bioacoustics—which is accelerating exponentially and unveiling fascinating findings about communication across the tree of life—is now approaching these animals and not asking, "Can they speak like humans?" but "Can they communicate complex information to one another? How are they doing so? What is significant to them?" And I would say that's a more biocentric approach or at the very least it's less anthropocentric.

Taking a bigger view, I think it's also important to acknowledge that listening to nature, "deep listening," has a long and venerable tradition. It's an ancient art that is still practiced in an unmediated form. There are long-standing Indigenous traditions of deep listening that are deeply attuned to nonhuman sounds. So if we combine digital listening—which is opening up vast new worlds of nonhuman sound and decoding that sound with artificial intelligence—with deep listening, I believe that we are on the brink of two important discoveries. The first is language in nonhumans. And that's a very controversial statement, which we can dig into. And the second is: I believe we're at the brink of interspecies communication.

Q: What sort of technology is enabling these breakthroughs?

A: Digital bioacoustics relies on very small, portable, lightweight digital recorders, which are like miniature microphones that scientists are installing everywhere from the Arctic to the Amazon. You can put these microphones on the backs of turtles or whales. You can put them deep in the ocean, [put them] on the highest mountaintop, attach them to birds. And they can record sound continuously, 24/7, in remote places where scientists cannot easily reach, even in the dark and without the disruption that comes from introducing human observers in an ecosystem.

That instrumentation creates a data deluge, and that is where artificial intelligence comes in—because the same natural language processing algorithms that we are using to such great effect in tools such as Google Translate can also be used to detect patterns in nonhuman communication.

Q: What's an example of these communication patterns?

A: In the bat chapter where I discuss the research of Yossi Yovel, there's a particular study in which he monitored [nearly two] dozen Egyptian fruit bats for two and a half months and recorded ... [their] vocalizations. His team then adapted a voice recognition program to analyze [15,000 of] the sounds, and the algorithm correlated specific sounds with specific social interactions captured via videos—such as when two bats fought over food. Using this, the researchers were able to classify the majority of bats' sounds. That is how Yovel and other researchers such as Gerry Carter have been able to determine that bats have much more complex language than we previously understood. Bats argue over food; they actually distinguish between genders when they communicate with one another; they have individual names, or "signature calls." Mother bats speak to their babies in an equivalent of "motherese." But whereas human mothers raise the pitch of their voices when talking to babies, mother bats lower the pitch—which elicits a babble response in the babies

58

that learn to "speak" specific words or referential signals as they grow up. So bats engage in vocal learning.

That's a great example of how deep learning is able to derive these patterns from [this] instrumentation, all of these sensors and microphones, and reveal to us something that we could not access with the naked human ear. Because most of bat communication is in the ultrasonic, above our hearing range, and because bats speak much faster than we do, we have to slow it down to listen to it, as well as reduce the frequency. So we cannot listen like a bat, but our computers can. And the next insight is, of course, that our computers can also speak back to the bat. [The software produces] specific patterns and uses those to communicate back to the bat colony or to the beehive, and that is what researchers are now doing.

Q: How are researchers talking to bees?

A: The honeybee research is fascinating. A [researcher] named Tim Landgraf studies bee communication, which, as I mentioned earlier, is vibrational and positional. When honeybees "speak" to one another, it's their body movements, as well as the sounds, that matter. Now computers, and particularly deep-learning algorithms, are able to follow this because you can use computer vision, combined with natural language processing. They have now perfected these algorithms to the point where they're actually able to track individual bees, and they're able to determine what impact the communication of an individual might have on another bee. From that emerges the ability to decode honeybee language. We found that they have specific signals. [Researchers have given these signals] funny names. [Bees] toot; they quack. There's a "hush" or "stop" signal, a whooping "danger" signal. They've got piping [signals related to swarming] and begging and shaking signals, and those all direct collective and individual behavior.

The next step for Landgraf was to encode this information into a robot that he called RoboBee. Eventually, after seven or eight prototypes, Landgraf came up with a "bee" that could enter the hive, and it would essentially emit commands that the honeybees would obey. So Landgraf's honeybee robot can tell the other bees to stop, and they do. It can also do something more complicated, which is the very famous waggle dance—it's the communication pattern they use to convey the location of a nectar source to other honeybees. This is a very easy experiment to run, in a way, because you put a nectar source in a place where no honeybees from the hive have visited, you then instruct the robot to tell the honeybees where the nectar source is, and then you check whether the bees fly there successfully. And indeed they do. This result only happened once, and scientists are not sure why it worked or how to replicate it. But it is still an astounding result.*

This raises a lot of philosophical and ethical questions. You could imagine such a system being used to protect honeybees—you could tell honeybees to fly to safe nectar sources and not polluted ones that had, let's say, high levels of pesticides. You could also imagine this could be a tool to domesticate a previously wild species that we have only imperfectly domesticated or to attempt to control the behavior of other wild species. And the insights about the level of sophistication and the degree of complex communication in nonhumans raises some very important philosophical questions about the uniqueness of language as a human capacity.

Q: What impact is this technology having on our understanding of the natural world?

A: The invention of digital bioacoustics is analogous to the invention of the microscope. When [Dutch scientist Antonie] van Leeuwenhoek started looking through his microscopes, he discovered the microbial world..., and that laid the foundation for countless future breakthroughs. So the microscope enabled humans to see anew with both our eyes and our imaginations. The analogy here is that digital bioacoustics, combined with artificial intelligence, is like a planetary-scale hearing aid that enables us to listen anew with both our prosthetically enhanced ears and our imagination. This is slowly opening our minds not only to the wonderful sounds that nonhumans make but to a fundamental set of questions about the so-called divide between humans and nonhumans, our relationship to other species. And [it's] also opening up new ways to think about conservation and our relationship to the planet. It's pretty profound.

Editor's Note (2/7/23): This paragraph was edited after posting to clarify that the described result of the RoboBee experiment only happened once.

About the Author

Sophie Bushwick is an associate editor covering technology at Scientific American.

Section 3: Animal Psychology and Behavior

Many Animals Can Think Abstractly

By Andrea Anderson

Our knack for language helps us structure our thinking. Yet the ability to wax poetic about trinkets, tools or traits may not be necessary to think about them abstractly, as was once suspected. A growing body of evidence suggests nonhuman animals can group living and inanimate things based on less than obvious shared traits, raising questions about how creatures accomplish this task.

In a study published last fall in the journal *PeerJ*, for example, Oakland University psychology researcher Jennifer Vonk investigated how well four orangutans and a western lowland gorilla from the Toronto Zoo could pair photographs of animals from the same biological groups.

Vonk presented the apes with a touch-screen computer and got them to tap an image of an animal—for instance, a snake—on the screen. Then she showed each ape two side-by-side animal pictures: one from the same category as the animal in the original image and one from another—for example, images of a different reptile and a bird. When they correctly matched animal pairs, they received a treat such as nuts or dried fruit. When they got it wrong, they saw a black screen before beginning the next trial. After hundreds of such trials, Vonk found that all five apes could categorize other animals better than expected by chance (although some individuals were better at it than others). The researchers were impressed that the apes could learn to classify mammals of vastly different visual characteristics together—such as turtles and snakes—suggesting the apes had developed concepts for reptiles and other categories of animals based on something other than shared physical traits.

Dogs, too, seem to have better than expected abstract-thinking abilities. They can reliably recognize pictures of other dogs, regardless of breed, as a study in the July 2013 *Animal Cognition* showed. The results surprised scientists not only because dog breeds vary so widely in appearance but also because it had been unclear whether dogs could routinely identify fellow canines without the advantage of smell and other senses. Other studies have found feats of categorization by chimpanzees, bears and pigeons, adding up to a spate of recent research that suggests the ability to sort things abstractly is far more widespread than previously thought.

There is still some question as to whether such visual categorization experiments reflect truly abstract thinking by animals, says Vonk, who noted that further work is needed to untangle the tricks various animals use in classification challenges. "I suspect the different species use different means of solving the task," she notes.

About the Author

Andrea Anderson is a science journalist based in Canada. She has written for Audubon, Discover *and* Nature Medicine.

We Are Not the Same (& That Is Fine): Different Approaches to Animal Behavior

By DNLee

I'm in full throttle Research mode and as I am oft to do – I think very deeply about the meaning and purpose of my tests. My ever-evolving research philosophy is definitely a very whole organism approach. The whole animal is my subject. In my care, the whole animal is my responsibility, not just the data it yields me. I put my mind space in that of the animal. *What is life? What am I doing? Why do I need to do it? Why am I doing it?* Trained very heavily in ecology and evolutionary biology the answers are simple—I am alive. I am here, now. I need to survive. I need to reproduce.

Experiments are how I "read my subject's mind". *What are they doing? Why are they doing it? What is the outcome?* Unlike people, I can't simply ask them to tell me what they are doing and why? (And heck, even people lie.) So, I have the amazing and challenging job to design experiments that ask mutually exclusive questions. Some of the most thorough and extensive behavior research has been conducted in laboratories by psychologists, behavioral pharmacologists, and physiologists.

First, some background. Animal Behavior is one of the oldest fields of science inquiry. Traditional cultures have oral, written, and illustrative accounts of animal behavior that far outstretch the modern Western definition of science. However, a student interested in Animal Behavior study today could follow one of four main paths to a career in behavior: Anthropology, Ecology, Psychology, Physiology.

We may study different species of animals. Or we may study the same species, but for completely different purposes, asking very different questions. How Ecologists "see" and study behavior is fundamentally different than how psychologists or physiologists study behavior; and how Anthropologists study behavior is very different than the rest. One major distinguishing feature of Anthropology is the relationship between the researcher and the subject. Anthropologists often embed themselves with their subjects in order to fully understand them. Think Jane Goodall approach. My experience with this approach is limited and I will spend the rest of the post discussing the remaining three avenues to animal behavior.

In Ecology animal subjects are the subject of interest. Questions are asked to understand how they survive, disperse, interact with conspecifics and other organisms in their communities, how they adjust/adapt to the environment and human intervention. Related fields include Behavioral Ecology, Ethology, Natural History.

In Psychology animal subjects are of interest because they (usually) serve as proxies of human behavior. Questions are asked to identify patterns and correlations of their behavior to help us understand more about our own or to identify general patterns in behavior across many species. Related fields include Clinical Psychology, Experimental Psychology, Psychobiology, Neurobehavior.

In Physiology animal subjects can be the subject of interest or a model for human or wider taxa questions. Questions are asked to understand how changes in the animal's system (internal physical, biochemical, neurological, reproductive, digestive, hormonal, etc.) impact behavior and vice versa. Related fields include Behavioral Pharmacology, Biomedical research, Reproductive Physiology, Neurobehavior.

Rodents are a commonly studied by professionals of all three fields. However, the growing popularity of Biomedical Research (and the declining popularity of natural history) has really shaped expectations about what it means to study animal behavior, both among the public and those who are researchers. When the average person thinks of a rodent subject, they think Lab Rats or Mice and for good reason. They are the most frequently used subjects for various types of research. A lot of important science happens in the lab, but the lab isn't the only place where science happens.

Pros and Cons of Lab vs Field Experiments

The Lab is clean. You can really isolate variables and design experiments to get to the minutia of inputs to behavior. Mechanism based behavior studies are especially keen on lab experiments: physiology, neurobiology. Development has definitely gained so much from super-controlled experiments that are able to observe and track changes in reproduction and embryology and more.

The Field is authentic. You get an uncut, unfiltered, front seat ticket to animal behavior. Understanding the what (Function) and why (Evolution) of how animals behave becomes more clear. *The context of the behavior is as essential as the behavior itself.* But all of this "context" makes for a tangly mess. Sorting out variables is hard, hard, hard.

Which makes what I do and how I study animal behavior challenging and exciting. I straddle the fences. I do a bit of both: Lab and Field based work. I apply psychological methods to examine animal behavior under ethological contexts. I intentionally focus on ethological questions (ecology approach) of animal behavior, but I often track (minimal) physiological changes in my subjects. I want to know about the animal, it's natural state, it's essence if you will. But I need to be able to identify what is happening with the animals. I need to tune out all of the noise of the environment and get a clear picture of what an animal is doing. This means I need to bring them into the lab, a controlled environment to get a good look at them and observe them. To aid in this "examination" I use tools designed by psychologists to examine single or small suites of behavior. Thanks to a very thorough literature I have the blueprints to a host of tests that are relatively easy to do and apparatuses that are easy to assemble or build.

But the tests are just tools, not the machinery proper of my outfit. That's because I am often working with completely different species and asking fundamentally different questions than the creators of those experiments. I see behavior differently. For me, the behavior is my focus, for behavioral pharmacologists, for example, the behavior is the result of a modification made in the animal. Moreover, field research and working with wild animals is altogether different than working in a lab with domesticated animals.

Wild animals are just that—wild. They scamper, bite, lunge. (Whatever shenanigans you think laboratory/domesticated/pet shop style/farm type animals do, I assure you that the wild varieties are faster, wilier, and more agile.) Wild animals are dirty—yes with actual dirt, but often have a host of pathogens and parasites that they've inherited since birth, maybe before. Field research is riskier—both in the physical risks researchers take to do their work. Exposure to Dengue-Malaria infested mosquitoes, Leptospirosis-tainted urine, tape/round/hookworm-infested poop, snakes, predators, hunters, poachers, you name it. Researchers spend weeks, even months to just access their animals and there's no guarantee they will encounter a single subject, let alone get a confident sample size of n=12 or more per treatment group. The stress of procuring and transferring animals to a lab is a nail biting time, too. Weeks (or months) of providing basic care and husbandry to an animal just to make sure it's in good health and condition before getting the okay to do any test.

For researchers, like me, who work with animal species that have no SOP (standard operating procedures), then you take the most cautious, conservative road to manipulations and observations. Because care and well-being of your subject is paramount. If something happens to one of my pouched rats, I don't have the option to order more from a catalog. But that's the why and how of what makes these different fields of animal behavior essential. We're exploring different questions for very, very different end points.

My end point is to identify the basic behavioral reactions of African Giant Pouched Rats to a suite of novel stimuli. That's it. How do they fare? And we want to know their basic, natural, not-antagonized behavioral responses so that we can get an idea of what they are like... because we don't know what they are like *at all.*

The views expressed are those of the author(s) and are not necessarily those of Scientific American.

Referenced

Coping and coping strategies: a behavioural view by Beat Wechsler, *Applied Animal Behaviour Science*, 1995, vol 43:123-134.

About the Author

DNLee is a biologist and she studies animal behavior, mammalogy, and ecology. She uses social media, informal experiential science experiences, and draws from hip hop culture to share science with general audiences, particularly under-served groups.

Do Dogs Have Mirror Neurons?

By Ádám Miklósi

The short answer is that dogs very likely possess mirror neurons, but we have no concrete proof just yet. Neuroscientist Giacomo Rizzolatti of the University of Parma in Italy and his colleagues discovered mirror neurons by accident during the 1990s, when they were studying motor neurons in rhesus monkeys. Rizzolatti and his co-workers found that certain neurons in the frontal and parietal cortex became active both when a monkey watched another monkey take food and when the monkey grabbed the food itself. They adopted the term "mirror neuron" to reflect the fact that these neurons fire in patterns that mimic others' actions.

Using functional brain imaging, neuroscientists have located brain areas with similar mirror function in humans. They believe that these neural structures may help us understand the intentions of another, to imitate and empathize with others, and perhaps even to process language. Additional evidence suggests that mirror neurons are not exclusive to primates or even mammals. Researchers have found dedicated mirror neurons in the brain of songbirds that fire both when the animal sings a particular tune and when it hears another songbird crooning a similar melody.

The presence of mirror neurons in other animals suggests that they may have an ancient evolutionary origin and play an important role in communication. So it seems entirely reasonable to hypothesize that dogs have mirror neurons, too. Dogs appear to imitate other dogs. And mirror neurons in dogs may support communication with humans; we will have to study dogs' brains more closely to find out.

Question submitted by Betty Sue, Easton, Me.

The World According to Dogs

By Julie Hecht

M ost of us do not understand dogs as well as we think we do. We assume we know things, but we often rely on old theories and frequently do not look at actual dog behavior. Instead we should try to think about life from the dog's perspective. The stories that follow highlight some of the more interesting discoveries that scientists have made about the minds behind all those cute canine faces.

The Meaning of Belly-Up

When a dog rolls onto its back during play, does the maneuver indicate submission, akin to a person crying "uncle," or does it signify something else altogether? A study by Kerri Norman, then at the University of Lethbridge in Alberta, and her colleagues there and at the University of South Africa comes down on the side of "something else." Their report appeared in 2015 in an issue of *Behavioural Processes* devoted to canine behavior.

Investigating what behaviors mean during dog-dog play is not new. For example, you have probably heard of play signals that help dogs to clarify play from not play. These signals indicate something like, "Hey, when I just bit you in the face, I didn't mean it like 'I'M BITING YOU IN THE FACE.' It was just for fun. See! Here's a play bow for additional clarity. All fun here!" Play signals may also include exaggerated, bouncy movements or presentation of a "play face"; they start or maintain play, and they occur around potentially ambiguous behaviors—such as a bite, tackle or mount—or anything that might be misconstrued as not playing. But not all behaviors that appear during play between dogs are as well studied.

Outside of play, rolling onto one's back is often seen as a submissive gesture that curtails or avoids aggression by another dog. In a classic 1967 paper in *American Zoologist*, Rudolf Schenkel of the University of Basel in Switzerland describes this so-called passive sumission as expressing "some kind of timidity and helplessness," like coming out with your hands up or waving a white flag.

Some have suggested that the rollover performed in dog-dog play is about preventing aggression. Owners observing playing dogs from the sidelines often take this a step further—the dog spending more time on its back is labeled "submissive" or "subordinate," whereas the dog on the top is "dominant."

But what if rolling over means something different during play? Norman and her colleagues wanted to know whether "rolling over onto the back and adopting a supine position" during play is an "act of submission" and serves to stop the interaction or hinder subsequent aggression. Or, they speculated, it might be essentially playful, "executed tactically, for combat purposes," to encourage play, avoid a play bite (defensive maneuver) or deliver a play bite (offensive maneuver).

The researchers collected data in two contexts: staged play sessions where a medium-sized female dog was paired with 33 new play partners of various breeds and sizes, and 20 YouTube videos where two dogs played together—half the videos paired similarly sized dogs, and the other half had dogs of different relative sizes.

Not all observed dogs rolled over during play, particularly in the staged play sessions, where only nine partners rolled over when playing. In the YouTube videos, 27 of the 40 dogs rolled over, and it occurred in both similarly sized and differently sized pairs. If your dog is not a roller during play, he is in good company.

For dogs that did roll over, what did it mean? The researchers examined all instances of the behavior to see whether rollovers were associated with submission—decreasing play, remaining passive, or being performed by the "smaller or weaker" partner—or were instead associated with the interactive, fun, combative nature of play, where rollovers preceded "launching an attack (offensive), evading a nape bite (defensive), rolling in front of a potential partner (solicitation) or rolling over in a nonsocial context (other)."

The findings are stark: the smaller of the two play partners was not more likely to roll over than the larger dog. Additionally, "most rollovers were defensive and none of the 248 rollovers was submissive." Most in-play rollovers in the study, the researchers found, were part of *play* fighting (meaning the fighting was itself playful, not *real* fighting).

But could it be that once dogs are on their back, submission kicks in? For example, a dog could go on its back to avoid a neck bite and then lie motionless, suggestive of passive submission. But that is not what the dogs did. Instead once on their back, dogs in the supine position both blocked playful bites and launched them at their partner.

Another way to think about rolling over in play is as a self-handicapping behavior that helps dogs of different sizes or sociabilities play together. Self-handicapping is instrumental to play, and it implies that a dog is tempering its behavior. For example, during play, dogs do not deliver bites at full force, and a larger dog might roll over to allow a smaller dog to jump on or mouth it. Some dogs will even use this behavior to invite bites and solicit play from another dog.

It is not safe, then, to assume that a dog sliding onto its back during play is essentially saying, "YOU CAME ON TOO STRONG" or "OKAY, YOU WON THIS ROUND!" In some contexts, this posture is certainly associated with fear or with defusing or preventing aggression, but the recent study reminds us that rolling over, as with many behaviors, does not have a single, universal meaning. Instead it is often just playful.

When a Dog Won't Play

You have probably heard the expression, "Life is short: play with your dog." "Okay!" you think, "I'll do it!" After all, dogs play together until they are exhausted. They also play with people, although good play is not always a given. Have you ever tried to play with a dog, and it just doesn't work? "The dog's not playing right," you may think. "This stinks."

Don't be so quick to blame the dog. Research suggests that it might be *you* who is not "playing right."

In 2001 animal welfare and behavior researcher Nicola Rooney, now at the University of Bristol in England, and her colleagues wanted to know whether dogs respond to people's play signals. In the study, volunteers played with their dog for five minutes in the comfort of their home, and the sessions were videotaped. Owners were asked to engage with their dog "as they usually did," but here is the key: they were not allowed to use objects or toys.

After the sessions, the researchers watched the videos and noted which behaviors owners used to initiate or maintain play. They identified 35 common play signals, including patting the floor, clapping, shoving, hitting or tapping the dog and, of course, play bowing. People also blew at dogs, barked at them and grabbed their paws. And who can forget my favorite behavior, "hand spider," where the "person moved their hand or fingers simulating movement of an insect or other creature."

Did dog owners' play signals instigate play? And more specifically, did the commonly used signals elicit play more often than the rarely used ones?

Of the 35 most common play signals, Rooney and her colleagues found that a signal's popularity "was not related to its success at initiating or sustaining play." For example, patting the floor was used most often, but play followed only 38 percent of the time. Other not so successful but commonly used invitations included scruffing the dog and clapping. Some things people did, including picking up or kissing the dog, failed to elicit play during any of the sessions.

All is not lost! A few behaviors were incredibly successful. The researchers found that giving chase and running away and lunging forward were associated with play 100 percent of the time. Signaling "up" (tapping one's chest to entice the dog to jump up), grabbing or holding a dog's paws, and play bowing also got great results.

The study's conclusion is somewhat somber: "We suggest that humans often use ineffective [play] signals." Instead of blaming dogs for not playing right, people could evaluate the effects of their own actions, acknowledging that certain signals are better at eliciting play than others.

Alexandra Protopopova, now at the Human-Animal Interaction Lab at Texas Tech University, and her colleagues at the Arizona State University Canine Science Collaboratory have highlighted a sad consequence of inept play signaling by humans: it can sabotage adoption of a dog from a shelter. The team found that when a potential adopter takes out a shelter dog for a one-on-one meet and greet, only two behavioral variables predicted whether that dog was leaving the shelter: lying in close proximity to the person and responding to the person's play solicitation. Dogs lying close to the person were about 14 times more likely to be adopted, and a dog who ignored a person's play initiation was unlikely to be adopted.

Taken together, these two studies paint a potentially scary picture for shelter dogs: people do not always use play signals that result in play, but people are unlikely to adopt a dog that does not respond to their signals. Nobody wins.

A subsequent study by Protopopova and her colleagues found that when potential adopters were explicitly told to play with a dog's preferred toy, not only did social play increase, but so, too, did adoption rate.

When I think about dogs in a shelter going up for their one-on-one interviews, I hope potential adopters cut them some slack and do not blame the dogs if they do not grasp overtures for play. The list of factors that could contribute to whether a dog will play with a new, strange human it just met is endless. On top of that, the shelter environment is often a weird, chaotic place, not exactly hospitable to having a fun time.

When meeting a dog for the first time, go slowly and keep your expectations in check. For shelter dogs, as with speed dating, a lot is riding on the first encounter. Reflect on your play behaviors just as much as you think about theirs.

Is That Really Guilt You See?

Live with a dog, and you have most likely met the "guilty look." You come home. The plants are knocked over, and soil is tracked all over the floor. The dog is abnormally still and averts its gaze as it thumps its tail slowly.

But does the dog feel responsible for the mess and sorry about having disobeyed your rules? That is hard to say. Research to date, including an open-access study published in 2015, suggests that the answer is no. Moreover, the findings reveal that scolding or punishing dogs will not necessarily decrease unwanted behavior.

Owners asked to describe a dog's guilty look comment that, in addition to potentially freezing, looking away and thumping their tails, the dog may try to look smaller and assume a nonthreatening pose. Some might lift a paw or approach the owner in a low posture. Others retreat.

It is tempting to think that if a dog acts much as we do when we feel guilty, then the dog must also understand that its behavior was wrong and feel guilty. Yet these are the same actions that animal behavior researchers and experts describe as reflective of submission, appeasement, anxiety or fear. Such displays are employed by social species, such as dogs and wild gray wolves, in many different contexts to reduce conflict, diffuse tension and reinforce social bonds.

When we investigators create experiments to better understand dogs' conceptual frameworks, we often find that although their actions might look much like those of people, their understanding of the situation might differ. In this case, it is possible that rather than guilt operating when your dog puts on a "guilty face," the pooch may actually be experiencing general anxiety or fear or a desire to avoid being on the wrong end of your anger or frustration.

In 2009 Alexandra Horowitz of Barnard College (and author of *Inside of a Dog: What Dogs See, Smell, and Know*) published a study in *Behavioural Processes* that explored the events preceding the seemingly guilty look. By varying both the dog's behavior (either eating or not eating a disallowed treat) and the owner's behavior (either scolding or not scolding), she was able to isolate what the look was associated with. She found that it did not appear more when the dogs had done something wrong. Instead it popped out in full form when the owner scolded. Horowitz further found that when dogs were reprimanded, the most exaggerated guilty look was displayed by the dogs that had not eaten the treat but were reprimanded anyway (because the owner thought the dog had eaten it). That means, for example, that in a multidog household, a dog could easily look guilty without ever having transgressed.

I found a similar result in a follow-up experiment that I conducted with Ádám Miklósi and Márta Gácsi of the Family Dog Project at Eötvös Loránd University in Budapest and published in 2012 in *Applied Animal Behaviour Science*. Dogs had the opportunity to break a rule (that food on a table is for humans and not dogs) while owners were out of the room. When the owners returned, dogs that ate were not more likely to look guilty than those that abstained. In this context, the guilty look was not present without a scolding owner. We also looked at whether owners are better able than others to tell when their dogs have been disobedient. Owners who had seen their companions adhere to the rule were not better at identifying that the dogs had transgressed in their absence.

"But wait!" the peanut gallery cries. "I have seen my dog act guilty before it is scolded." Owners often do interpret such behavior to mean that dogs "know" they have done wrong. This is a complicated issue, but findings to date suggest that dogs engage in guilty-seeming behavior when they sense that something will elicit an owner's displeasure and hope to avoid a breach in the relationship.

Ljerka Ostojić and Nicola Clayton of the University of Cambridge and Mladenka Tkalčić of the University of Rijeka in Croatia reported in 2015 in an open-access article in *Behavioural Processes* on whether a dog's guilty look could be triggered by environmental cues, such as the disappearance of a forbidden food. By using a manipulation somewhat similar to that of Horowitz, Ostojić and her colleagues found that the guilty look was not affected by the dog's own behavior (either eating or not eating the food) or whether the food was present or absent. In their experimental context, dogs did not display the guilty look in the absence of a scolding owner.

At the same time, the study does not exclude the possibility that in the home environment, owners may very well observe the infamous look prior to scolding. In the late 1970s a veterinarian in Wisconsin published a paper offering a clear example of fear masquerading as guilt. A dog called Nicki had taken to shredding paper in the owner's absence. To see if the dog's guilty-seeming behavior actually stemmed from guilt, the veterinarian had the owner shred paper, leave the house and return home. When the owner came back, Nicki looked "guilty," even though she had done nothing wrong. Dogs are incredibly sensitive to environmental and social cues. In this case, the dog apparently viewed the paper on the floor as a sign of a scolding to come.

"Evidence + Owner = Trouble," explains primatologist Frans de Waal, in *Good Natured: The Origins of Right and Wrong in Humans and Other Animals*. As a social species aiming to maintain relationships, dogs could show submissive displays before an owner scolds without the behavior indicating an apology or admittance of guilt. Instead these displays can aim to appease or pacify. And they certainly could have that effect: in one study, I found that nearly 60 percent of owners surveyed on a questionnaire reported that the "guilty look" led them to scold their dog less.

You may wonder why I and others harp on the misattribution of a sense of guilt in dogs. As I have said online in The Dodo, this is an issue about dog welfare: "When you get angry or forgive your 'guilty' dog for demolishing your house, you ignore deeper concerns that, if addressed, could reduce or eliminate those behavior problems. Was the dog bored? Scared? Anxious? Did something change in your routine that confused it? Sadly, scolding dogs often does not decrease future undesirable behavior. If anything, the 'guilty look' could just become more exaggerated over time as your confused companion enters an anxious cycle of destruction and appeasement."

Even worse, scolding a guilty-looking dog after the fact could give you a false sense of mutual understanding and the incorrect belief that you are punishing the bad behavior effectively. A punishment, by definition, decreases the behavior in the future. Unfortunately, studies find that scolding a "disobedient" dog, especially after it misbehaves, does not lead to a notable decrease in the "bad" behavior. A study from the late 1960s found that dogs reprimanded just 15 seconds after performing a "disallowed" behavior not only continued to perform the behavior in the future but did so while showing notable appeasement and fear-related behaviors.

Beratement after the fact does not work, and the guilty look is better interpreted as fear or appeasement. Best to just clean up the mess and think about how to avoid it in the future.

Why Dogs Like People

Do you ever wonder what makes some dogs so into us? Why at any moment Pluto might propel himself into Mickey's arms, giving Mickey a full-on scrub down with his tongue? Why some dogs want to meet everybody, whereas others would prefer you stay right where you are?

A 2014 study published in *PLOS ONE* by researchers led by Anna Kis and Melinda Bence, now at the Hungarian Academy of Sciences, researchers at the Family Dog Project at Eötvös Loránd University in Budapest and others used a novel method to explore the role that oxytocin plays in dogs' sociability toward humans.

Maybe you have heard oxytocin described as the "love hormone" because of its involvement in social interactions, stress relief and feelings of connectedness with other people. Spend time petting your dog, scratching Pluto's body and ears, and you are both apt to see increases in the oxytocin levels in your blood, indicating a positive experience for you both. Yet oxytocin is also not simple. Science writer Ed Yong points out in a 2012 *Slate* article: "The 'love hormone' fosters trust and generosity in some situations but envy and bias in others, and it can produce opposite effects in different people." Part of the story could be that variations in the gene that codes for the oxytocin receptor—the molecule that oxytocin binds to on nerve cells in the brain—mediate differences in social behavior.

To investigate whether Pluto's exuberance for Mickey and "people" in general is somehow associated with Pluto's genes, Kis and her colleagues took the following approach:

- Step 1. Get to know the dog oxytocin receptor (*OXTR*) gene. For this study, the researchers selected dogs from two popular breeds, German shepherds and Border collies, and extracted DNA by swabbing the insides of their cheeks. This process ultimately identified three variations of the *OXTR* gene, each of which comes in two forms, with the forms seemingly having different effects on behavior. The three variations, or "polymorphisms," have the incredibly easy names of *–212AG, 19131AG* and *rs8679684*.
- Step 2. Get a sense of how the dogs interact with people. More than 200 German shepherds and Border collies living as pets participated in a series of interactions with people. The tests investigated how dogs greeted both a known and an unknown person, how dogs responded to a stranger approaching in a threatening manner, and how dogs responded when their owner hid behind a large tree.
- Step 3. Bring dog genes and dog behavior together. The researchers examined whether there was a relation between the *OXTR* polymorphisms and the way the dogs interacted with people during the social tests. They were particularly interested in how readily dogs approached people, as well as the canines' level of friendliness.

Describing the results, Kis says that "the way dogs behave toward humans, at least among German shepherds and Border collies, is influenced by the oxytocin receptor gene." For example, when it came to the *–212AG* gene, both German shepherds and Border collies carrying the form, or allele, known as G showed less interest in being around people than did those with the allele called A, suggesting the effect was the same in both breeds.

Yet analysis of the genes *19131AG* and *rs8679684* revealed opposite trends in the two breeds. For example, in the *19131AG* polymorphism, the investigators report, "the presence of the A allele, as opposed to the G allele, was associated with higher friendliness scores in German Shepherds and lower friendliness scores in Border Collies." This opposite effect suggests that "other genetic and cellular mechanisms (unexplored in the present study) might play a role in the regulation of this behavior besides our candidate gene."

Overall, then, the study indicates that dog sociability toward people is related to the varieties in the *OXTR* gene they possess but that oxytocin is "part of a bigger system" contributing to dogs' feelings toward humans.

Next up for this line of research: replication and the exploration of possible molecular interactions that account for the effects that particular oxytocin receptor variants have on dogs' behavior toward people.

Beware the Fear

Knowing when a dog is happy is easy, but spotting fear is a lot harder, as Michele Wan, a certified applied animal behaviorist, and her colleagues showed in research examining whether people's perceptions of dogs' emotions vary according to experience. In the study, published in 2012 in *PLOS ONE*, volunteers—who were grouped as having little or no experience with dogs, having lived with a dog at some point, or working with dogs for more or less than 10 years—watched short video clips of dogs. Volunteers were asked to describe the dogs' emotional state and noted which body parts tipped them off. Because the videos had no sound, participants had to rely on behavior to label a dog as, say, fearful or happy. These videos were not just any videos. They had been prescreened by dog-behavior experts whose schooling or professional experience had trained them to make science-based assessments of animal behavior.

Happy dogs proved easiest to identify. Even people with little dog experience could watch a dog frolicking in the snow or rolling joyfully on its back and describe that dog as happy.

But fear was different. Study participants who were dog professionals did a better job identifying fear compared with both dog owners and people with little dog experience. "It did not matter whether the dog professionals were relative newcomers to the field, had worked with dogs for less than 10 years, or were longtime professionals with 10 or more years of experience," Wan adds. "They had the same proficiency in identifying fear."

One reason that the dog professionals did so much better could be that they looked at more dog body parts for clues, such as the eyes, ears, mouth and tongue, whereas nonprofessionals looked at fewer body parts and were less likely to tune into dogs' facial features.

Fortunately, you can learn how to notice and interpret subtle canine behaviors. Indeed, even if you live with the most happy-go-lucky dog on the planet, fear should still be on your radar, especially if your dog ever interacts with other dogs. Recognizing fear in another dog can help you know to give that dog space; the owner can take it from there.

What does fear look like? It can include a wide variety of body parts and postures. Wan and her colleagues explain that "fearful dogs are said to reduce their body size—crouching into a low posture, flattening their ears and holding their tails in a low position. Shaking, yawning, salivation, freezing, panting, paw lifting and vocalizing are examples of other behaviors that have been associated with fear in dogs."

It is possible to help dogs become less fearful. Noticing fear and related behaviors is the first step; identifying and modifying an animal's perception of fear-inducing stimuli is just as important. Picture a dog that is afraid of new people coming to the home, everyone from the postal delivery worker to your best friend. But now, when anyone comes to the home, the dog gets pieces of its most favorite food. Through counterconditioning, visitors gradually assume a new meaning as the dog associates people coming over with a good thing, in this case yummy food. As the dog's emotions shift, so, too, does its behavior—fearful postures fade away to reveal a dog anticipating something good, a dog essentially saying, "OMG!! A NEW PERSON IS HERE!! YES!!" A happy dog is born.

What Barks Say

Although at times your dog makes vocalizations that might be unwelcome, those sounds carry much information and meaning.

In recent years many studies have investigated the noises made by companion dogs.

One major finding: dogs bark differently in various contexts, and we can tell the difference. A 2004 study by Sophia Yin and Brenda McCowan in *Animal Behaviour* reported that "disturbance barks" (emitted in response to a stranger ringing the doorbell) sound different from "isolation barks" (when a dog is separated from an owner) and barks emitted during play. In each context, the acoustics differ: whereas disturbance barks are "relatively low-pitched, harsh barks with little variation in pitch or loudness," isolation barks are "higher pitched, more tonal and more frequency modulated than the disturbance barks," and play barks are "similar to the isolation barks except that they usually occurred in clusters rather than singly."

Instead of seeing barks as meaningless noise, pay attention. Banjo might be yipping because he is alone, or he may have noticed that someone uninvited is climbing in through your second-floor window.

Dog barks are full of information, but what about growls? Anna Taylor, now at the Queen's University (Ontario) Bader International Study Center in England, found that, unlike barks, many acoustic properties of growls in a play and aggressive context are alike. But aggressive growls were longer than play growls, and play growls had a shorter pause between growls. Although growls from different contexts can sound similar to human ears, Tamás Faragó and his colleagues at the Family Dog Project at Eötvös Loránd University in Budapest found that growls carry considerable meaning in dog-dog communication.

In a 2010 study published in *Animal Behaviour*, dogs were placed in a room with a bone; as they approached the bone, researchers played a recording of one of three different types of growls. Dogs responded to the "this is my food" growl by backing away from the bone and, for the most part, ignored the "go away stranger" and the play growls because those sounds were not relevant to the bone. All growls are not the same, and dogs know it.

Even though not all growls are associated with aggression, an aggressive growl should not be ignored. If you come across a situation where growling could be a sign of aggression, keep your cool, though. Jolanta Benal, author of the 2011 *The Dog Trainer's Guide to a Happy, Well-Behaved Pet (Quick and Dirty Tips)*, reminds: if you punish a dog for growling, you are essentially punishing it for giving a warning. Growling is a form of communication related to emotional or inner states in a particular context. If you want to decrease it, think about what is prompting it. The growling itself is not a problem.

When We're Angry, Dogs Get the Feels

Dog lovers may find it obvious that dogs pick up on our emotions. Attending to our emotional expression—in our faces, behavior or even smell—helps them live intimately by our side.

"Dogs get us," we say. End of story. Yet what about their side of the story? If dogs attend to our emotions—particularly those we wear on our faces—how might dogs feel when they see our different emotions?

An answer to this question arose almost by accident. In 2015 Corsin A. Müller and his colleagues at the University of Veterinary Medicine, Vienna, published a study that sought to determine whether dogs can discern happy and angry expressions in human faces, as opposed to relying on other cues (their finding: yes, dogs can get this information from our faces alone).

Because of the study design, the researchers could also peer into how dogs might feel about our emotions. In the study, pet dogs saw images of happy or angry human faces on a computer screen. To get a treat, the dogs had to approach and nose-touch a particular image on the screen. These are dogs. They can do this. Nose-touch for a treat? Yes, please!

But when viewing the angry faces, the researchers noticed something odd. Dog performance was affected by whether they saw happy or angry expressions. During the initial training, dogs seeing the angry expression took longer to learn to approach and nose-touch the image for a treat than did dogs that saw the happy expression. In other words, dogs were less inclined to approach and nose-touch angry faces, even though doing so would yield a treat.

"Why would I approach an angry person? That makes no sense," a dog might think. Through past experiences with people, dogs could come to view the angry expression as aversive. The researchers suggest that dogs "had to overcome their natural tendency to move away from aversive (or threatening) stimuli."

Reluctance to approach is only one way to assess how dogs perceive our emotions. To tackle the same question, a study published in January 2018 in *Behavioural Processes* turned to a subtle and often overlooked behavior that you might spot more often after today.

Natalia Albuquerque of the University of Lincoln in England and the University of São Paulo in Brazil and her colleagues presented dogs with images of angry and happy faces. The researchers found that when dogs looked at images of angry human faces, they were more likely to mouth-lick than when they saw happy human faces. And we are not talking about "yum ... food" mouth-licking.

Mouth-licking, the scientists say, "is believed to be an indicator of short-term (or acute) stress responses." This behavior has been identified in stressful contexts such as when a dog is startled by a loud noise or when a dog is alone and experiencing separation-related issues. In social situations, a quick in/out of the tongue may suggest emotional conflict and could be accompanied by other subtle behaviors that indicate, "Umm... interact? No, I'd rather keep my distance, thanks." Licking is also commonly found in appeasement or pacifying contexts.

Unlike trembling, whining, excessive barking and panting—which owners more regularly identify as stress-related—people are less likely to identify subtle behaviors such as looking away, turning the head, yawning and lip-licking as possible indicators of dog discomfort.

Now it should make more sense why the researchers looked at dog mouth-licking: "As the mouth-licking behavior was associated with the viewing of negative faces," they explain, "it is likely that these negative emotional visual stimuli were perceived as aversive by the dogs."

A canine's extended tongue should be on dog lovers' radar. To clarify, we are not talking about just any tongue extension, such as those associated with food, or a happy dog's lolling tongue, or a tongue engaged in licking someone. Though inconsistently labeled and described in the literature, the tongue extension we are discussing is generally described as an in/out of the tongue that may (or may not) go over the nose. Out in the real world, dogs may display this type of tongue extension in concert with behaviors such as lifting a paw, yawning, turning the head and looking away, being still, moving away or making the body smaller. Seems like we are going to need a bigger radar.

"If a dog starts tongue-flicking and turning his head when I reach to pet him, I'm going to pay a lot of attention to it and probably change my own behavior," offers Patricia McConnell, a certified applied animal behaviorist.

So dogs do indeed attend to our emotional expression. That is our part of the story. Their part of the story is written in their behavior.

About the Author

Julie Hecht is a Ph.D. student studying dog behavior and writes the Dog Spies blog at ScientificAmerican.com.

1 Sneeze, 1 Vote among African Wild Dogs

By Jason G. Goldman

When is a sneeze more than a sneeze? For African wild dogs, it turns out that sneezes are a form of voting. Gather a bunch of wild dogs together and a sneezing chorus becomes a way of implementing democratic decision-making.

African wild dogs, also known as painted dogs thanks to their colorful, splotchy coats, are known for highly energetic greeting rituals called social rallies.

> "It's kind of flat and shrubby in Botswana where these dogs are living. So they spend all day sleeping usually in the shade in dog piles without 20 meters of one another."

> Botswana Predator Conservation Trust and Brown University researcher Hallie Walker.

> "And so once one dog wants to leave and go hunting, they'll get up from rest and assume this kind of stereotyped posture...I think the easiest way to imagine it is when you get home from work and your dog is really excited to see you; they do that but with each other."

She and her colleagues noticed that dogs would sneeze a lot near the end of their social rallies. At first, they thought the dogs were simply clearing out their dusty airways, but a closer look revealed something more complex.

Walker and her team recorded the details of 68 social rallies from five different wild dog packs in Botswana. And the more sneezes they counted, the more likely it was that the pack would move off and begin hunting. One sneeze, one vote. The finding is in the *Proceedings of the Royal Society B*. [Reena H. Walker et al., Sneeze to leave: African wild dogs (*Lycaon pictus*) use variable quorum thresholds facilitated by sneezes in collective decisions]

It's not a perfectly democratic system though. When the dominant pair of dogs was involved in the sneeze-fest, the pack only required a few sneezes before they took off. But if the dominant pair was not involved, an average of 10 sneezes was needed to decide the matter. Seems that some votes carry more weight than others.

African wild dogs are highly endangered—there may be just 1,400 fully grown adults left in the wild. Walker argues that the more we can understand their behavior and pack dynamics, the better positioned we can be to protect them.

> "Anything that we learn more about their decision making can help us manage them better and anticipate those decisions. So that even something as simple as understanding...how they make decisions amongst themselves will help conservationists anticipate those decisions and try to prevent any human–wildlife conflict."

—Jason G. Goldman

[The above text is a transcript of this podcast.]

About the Author

Jason G. Goldman is a science journalist based in Los Angeles. He has written about animal behavior, wildlife biology, conservation, and ecology for Scientific American, Los Angeles *magazine, the* Washington Post, *the* Guardian, *the* BBC, Conservation *magazine, and elsewhere. He contributes to* Scientific American's *"60-Second Science" podcast, and is co-editor of* Science Blogging: The Essential Guide *(Yale University Press). He enjoys sharing his wildlife knowledge on television and on the radio, and often speaks to the public about wildlife and science communication.*

New Research Questions "Pawedness" in Dogs

By Julie Hecht

I'm right handed. Utensils, pens, pencils, and of course my toothbrush are all operated by my right hand. Like roughly 90 percent of people, my left hand simply isn't cut out for much on its own.

Dogs, outfitted with paws not hands, also appear to prefer one paw over the other. In dogs, paw laterality—or paw preference—is explored not with forks or pencils, but with more dog-appropriate motor tasks. Studies have asked which paw dogs use to reach toward food or which paw they use to remove something from their body, like a blanket. Researchers have even checked which paw dogs first lift to walk down a step and which paw they "give" when asked to "give" paw. To date, it has been assumed that, like us, dogs have a "hand" preference.

But Deborah Wells, a longtime laterality researcher, wondered if something was missing. Studies of paw preference typically use only one test to investigate paw preference. As a result, it is unclear whether "dogs harbor consistent paw preferences" or, on the other hand (ha!), whether paw preference instead might be task-specific. Maybe a dog consistently reaches for food with the right paw, but is more likely to lift the left front paw to walk down a step.

Wells and colleagues at the Animal Behaviour Center, Queen's University, Belfast, took the natural next step (ha again!). They tested 32 pet dogs on four different paw preference tests to see whether dog paw preference was consistent across tests. To check preferences over time, a subset was tested 6 months later. This research was recently published in *Behavioural Processes*.

All dogs participated in four tests: The Kong Ball Test assessed which paw dogs used to stabilize a Kong that had food in it; the Tape Test assessed which paw dogs used to try and remove a small piece of tape stuck to their nose; the Lift Paw Test assessed which paw dogs lifted to "give" a paw; and the First-Step Test assessed which paw dogs first lifted when walking down a step. For each test, multiple instances of paw use were recorded to explore preference strength and direction.

Wells had been on the right track. Instead of dogs showing consistent paw preference—always using the left or right paw in each test—paw preference was instead task-specific. A dog might use the right paw in the Kong test but lift the left to take a step. The findings, the researchers suggest, "do not therefore support the interpretation of true 'pawedness' in the dog." At the same time, test-specific paw preferences seemed stable over time, apart from the Tape Test, which the researchers do not recommend for future laterality studies. (Dogs were more "frantic" in their movements to remove the tape and more likely to use both paws.)

If the purpose of motor-bias research is not yet clear, I assure you laterality researchers are not trying to organize a well-attended round of hokey pokey. Instead, researchers are interested in motor bias because the relationship between motor bias and brain lateralization can have animal welfare implications. For example, animals showing left-limb preference tend to be more active in the right hemisphere of the brain, and these individuals "show stronger fear responses than right-limbed animals, which tend to be left-hemisphere dominant." An earlier study by Wells and colleagues found that left-pawed dogs were more "negative or 'pessimistic' in their cognitive outlook than right-pawed or ambilateral individuals." But the current study might put a damper on efforts to connect paw preference with broader animal welfare implications. If paw preference in dogs is not consistent between tasks, the researchers explain, "the study raises questions as to which test of paw preference is the most appropriate to employ."

The views expressed are those of the author(s) and are not necessarily those of Scientific American.

Referenced

Wells, D. L., Hepper, P. G., Milligan, A. D. S., & Barnard, S. (2018). Stability of motor bias in the domestic dog, *Canis familiaris. Behavioural Processes*, 149, 1–7.

About the Author

Julie Hecht is a Ph.D. student studying dog behavior and writes the Dog Spies blog at ScientificAmerican.com.

Small Dogs Aim High When They Pee

By Julie Hecht

Betty McGuire is no stranger to dog urine. If you live with a dog, neither are you. I'm guessing your dog pee story is probably one of waiting: waiting while your dog checks out another dog's pee, or waiting while your dog leaves a deposit. And who hasn't experienced the occasional, "Ack! Why did you pee there?!?" followed by a cleaning session. But if you've ever gazed at a peeing dog and asked yourself any number of "Why" questions, Betty McGuire is the person for you.

McGuire, a researcher and senior lecturer at the Department of Ecology and Evolutionary Biology at Cornell University, studies dog urinary behavior. Her research looks at the complex amalgam of dog factors—like age, sex, reproductive status, height, and body size—that contribute to how and where dogs pee. For over 10 years, McGuire and her colleagues have shown there's not one way to look at a peeing dog. Her scientific studies have tackled topics like dog urinary posture—including the squat, squat-raise, arch-raise, combination, and yes even the handstand (which I covered here)—motor laterality, i.e., which hind-limb dogs lift when peeing, and scent-marking behaviors like ground scratching.

McGuire conducts much of her work in collaboration with local SPCA animal shelters. "Our research provides shelter dogs with additional opportunities for exercise and socialization, as well as chances to display species-typical behaviors," she explains on her website. Also, animal shelters are great places to watch a lot of dogs pee.

Even if you don't think much about dog pee, McGuire's latest question has probably crossed your mind: when a dog pees on an object like a tree or a fire hydrant, do some dogs aim their pee to land "higher up" on the vertical surface than other dogs? Does what I'll call Pee Height—where the urine lands—accurately represent the size of the urinator? ("The Urinator" must be the name of a rejected Marvel superhero.) McGuire and colleagues' study was recently published in the *Journal of Zoology*.

First, the basics: Adult male dogs tend to raise a back leg to pee; juveniles tend to assume a lean-forward posture; and females tend to squat. (Of course, if you're thinking, "Not my dog!" you're right. Individual dogs can deviate from these trends, as I cover elsewhere). Dog researchers love dog pee (for research purposes only, they swear) because dog urine isn't merely for excretion. It carries social information about individuals, like sex, age, and reproductive status. Pee Height, too, might provide information to other dogs. The hind-leg raise attracts attention because, in this position, dogs have the most control over urine placement.

To explore whether a dog's Pee Height reflects the dog's size, McGuire and colleagues recorded adult male mixed-breed dogs, both intact and neutered, out on walks at two animal shelters. The researchers excluded juveniles who might not raise a leg and seniors who might not raise due to orthopedic issues. The researchers accounted for factors like body size—height and mass—and used the videos to measure raised-leg angle during urination as well as urine mark height (Pee Height).

The researchers found that in some cases, Pee Height accurately reflected the size of the urinator. This means if you're a dog checking out pee on a fire hydrant, the height of the pee you're sniffing could tell you about the size of the dog who left it.

But small dogs didn't fit the pattern. McGuire and colleagues found that, on average, small dogs raised their legs *higher* when peeing, which increased their angles, and resulted in their pee hitting higher than the dogs' height might predict. There is no better use of trigonometry. "Thus, even though height of urine mark does reflect size of signaler in part," the researchers observe, "small dogs seem to 'cheat' by using larger raised-leg angles to deposit higher urine marks, thereby exaggerating their size."

If you think you're going to read this piece without an exceptional visual example, you are incorrect. Meet Patches. When Patches pees, his leg begins at 115 degrees to produce a urine mark with a Pee Height of 15.3 cm. Then, *during the same urination*—and without shifting his planted legs or moving closer to the tree—Patches raises his leg higher to 120 degrees to achieve a Pee Height of 17.8 cm. Bravo, Patches. Bravo.

Exactly why small dogs aim high remains to be seen. One hypothesis involves the intersection of two concepts: dogs use pee as part of communication, and small dogs might engage in more indirect forms of communication because direct social interactions could be more costly for them. For example, in a 2017 study, McGuire and Bemis observed that small dogs urine mark more frequently than large dogs, spreading themselves around more than large dogs. And by increasing their Pee Height, what might be happening is that small dogs are using pee to exaggerate their own size and possibly aid in avoiding conflict.

Another potential explanation is that small dogs might perform these leg lifting exercises in an attempt to "over mark"—pee on top of another dog's pee. Mammals, including dogs, use over marking to cover others' deposits with their own scent, and dogs of all sizes seem to over mark. Of course, the higher a dog's Pee Height, the more urine a dog can potentially over mark. Due to their natural height advantage, larger dogs don't have to work their leg much to over mark, while smaller dogs need to limber up. Maybe attempting to over mark is what prompts smaller dogs to perform these acrobatics in the first place, a possibility that should be explored—and controlled for—in future studies, the researchers add.

There's also the possibility that larger dogs might be physically constrained from lifting their legs higher. Because dogs often lean in the opposite direction of the target during raised-leg urinations, larger dogs might be limited in how high they can lift without toppling over. No one wants to fall over mid-pee. Not even dogs.

And then there are the dogs who lift and miss. The researchers note that "dogs sometimes miss targets, especially poles and tree trunks of small diameter..." It remains to be seen if there are any trends or patterns in who lifts and misses. If social meaning is being attached to where deposits "land," but some deposits don't "land," how might poor aim affect dog social interactions? Do they even know they missed?

Because McGuire's study was observational, experimental studies exploring why small dogs tend to aim high, and how dogs respond to urine encountered at different heights, is a much-anticipated next step.

The views expressed are those of the author(s) and are not necessarily those of Scientific American.

Referenced

McGuire, B., Olsen, B., Bemis, K. E., & Orantes, D. (2018). Urine marking in male domestic dogs: honest or dishonest? *Journal of Zoology*, First published online: 25 July 2018

About the Author

Julie Hecht is a Ph.D. student studying dog behavior and writes the Dog Spies blog at ScientificAmerican.com.

Section 4: Quirks of the Human-Pet Bond

Cuteness Inspires Aggression

By Carrie Arnold

Whether we are pinching the cheeks of an adorable toddler or enveloping a beloved pet in a bear hug, most of us have experienced the strange drive to give something cute a gigantic squeeze. New research by two Yale University psychologists details how the sight of something cute brings out our aggressive side. Rebecca Dyer and Oriana Aragon investigated "cute aggression" by showing study participants slide shows of either cute, funny, or normal animal photographs. As they watched, the participants held bubble wrap. The researchers, attempting to mimic the common desire to squeeze cute things, told subjects to pop as many or as few bubbles as they wished. People watching the cute slide show popped significantly more bubbles than those viewing the funny or control pictures, according to results presented at the Society for Personality and Social Psychology annual meeting in New Orleans. "Some things are so cute that we just can't stand it," Dyer concludes.

Cute aggression's prevalence does not mean that people actually want to harm cuddly critters, Aragon explains. Rather the response could be protective, or it could be the brain's way of tamping down or venting extreme feelings of giddiness and happiness. The scientists are currently conducting additional studies to determine what drives the need to squeeze.

About the Author

Carrie Arnold is an independent public health reporter based in Virginia.

We Surrender Our Dogs. Help Scientists Understand Why.

By Julie Hecht

"We would love to tell you that every dog can flourish in every home, but the truth is that, no matter what you do, sometimes a dog and family are not a good fit."

~ Patricia McConnell and Karen London,
Love Has No Age Limit: Welcoming an
Adopted Dog into Your Home

My first dog, Brandy, was from an animal shelter. While I have a story I tell myself about her life before me, I really don't know whether she was a stray or whether she had another home before mine. Maybe you have surrendered a dog. Maybe someone you know has. Maybe you live with a dog who used to live elsewhere. Companion animal relinquishment is real, and it is a reality that is not well understood. Now, with help from people all over the world, scientists are hoping to change that.

Today we focus on dog relinquishment, "the voluntary surrendering or giving up of a pet dog to another individual, party, or organization." Relinquishment is part of the life story of many companion animals, the reasons for which might be complicated and personal. Feelings of guilt, shame, or embarrassment can plague people who have surrendered a pet. Some might feel angry, others conflicted or confused. Some might feel confident in their decision. The quest to understand companion dog relinquishment continues.

The American Society for the Prevention of Cruelty to Animals (ASPCA) estimates that approximately 7.6 million dogs and cats enter United States animal shelters each year as strays or owner surrenders. But these estimates are only part of the story; these estimates only look at the United States and are not comprehensive of the worldwide phenomenon. Additionally, these estimates do not include the general state of companion animal relinquishment which also includes people giving pets to groups or organizations other than animals shelters—like rescue groups or foster care organizations—or people relinquishing pets to another person.

Researchers at The University of Lincoln are conducting an international, online survey on the factors leading people to relinquish a pet dog. If you or someone you know has ever surrendered a companion dog, the researchers are hoping for your participation.

Karen Griffin, a PhD student at The University of Lincoln, Animal Behaviour Cognition and Welfare Team (Twitter), is leading the online survey. She explains, "Pet dog relinquishment is a topic on which there has been quite limited academic research thus far, most likely due to its sensitive and emotional nature." With this international survey, Griffin hopes to understand the "factors that lead to a pet dog staying in a home as well as the factors that lead to a pet dog being relinquished."

Griffin's online survey differs from earlier studies investigating pet dog relinquishment. Many studies are in-person interviews or questionnaires that focus on owners who are actively surrendering a pet to an animal shelter. Interviews generally take place at the time of surrender—a potentially emotional time—and some people are not interviewed due to their agitated state. Additionally, responses could be skewed by the act of surrender. For example, Zazie Todd (Twitter) who maintains the Companion Animal Psychology blog, reviewed a 2013 study on why people surrender dogs to animal shelters. In the study, experimenters interviewed owners who were either dropping a dog off at the shelter for surrender or who were at the shelter to have their dog vaccinated. In her coverage of the study, Todd explains that not all owners were approached by the experimenters: "Some people were not approached to take part because their dogs seemed to be aggressive, and the experimenter would have had to hold them while the owner completed the questionnaire. In addition, if relinquishing owners seemed particularly upset or arrived requesting euthanasia of the dog, they were not asked to take part, so as not to exacerbate their distress. It is possible this had an effect on the results."

An online survey is a potentially less-invasive way to explore a difficult or emotion-laden topic. Anyone who has voluntarily relinquished a dog can take part in this 15 to 20 minute survey on their own time and share details that might have been difficult to share in the moment. Like previous studies, the survey can reach people in different locations (such as urban, rural, and suburban), and the survey can also draw international responses.

The current survey is also more broad because it aims to gather feedback not only from people who have surrendered a pet dog to an animal shelter, but from anyone who has voluntarily surrendered a dog to another individual or organization.

Griffin and her colleagues hope to gain a deeper understanding of the factors behind dog surrender. As Griffin explains, "Previous studies have largely focused on static descriptions of the dog owner—such as family size and structure, living arrangements, and type of employment—all of which are prone to change during the time the dog is in the [domestic] environment. Changes in such things are often given as risk factors for pet dog relinquishment. However, they do not inevitably necessitate relinquishment, so this study hypothesizes that other causes are at play."

I asked Griffin if she thinks it is difficult for people to openly discuss surrendering a companion dog, and whether she thinks a social stigma is attached. Her response reminded me that this phenomenon can be more complex than I had imagined.

"Yes, I think this can be a very difficult subject to discuss for anybody who has ever surrendered a dog. While I do believe that there is some social stigma associated with it, I don't believe that it's the only reason why it's a sensitive subject. I think that the circumstances surrounding the relinquishment can be difficult or painful in and of themselves (e.g. a divorce), so revisiting this event can be hard. I also think that it can be filled with particularly challenging emotions like regret, shame, or guilt; people may feel this although the surrender was voluntary. I think the social stigma reinforces these negative feelings.

"The goal is by no means to place any judgment. Many years ago, long before dogs were my field of study or profession, I relinquished a dog. I am still ridden with guilt and shame; it was a very dark event in my life, and one I most certainly would not be eager to revisit if asked, so I absolutely understand that I am asking a lot of others to do the same. I sincerely hope that anybody who chooses to participate will understand the benefits that can be gained from more research and greater understanding of this topic."

The views expressed are those of the author(s) and are not necessarily those of Scientific American.

Referenced

Kwan J.Y. (2013). Owner Attachment and Problem Behaviors Related to Relinquishment and Training Techniques of Dogs, *Journal of Applied Animal Welfare Science*, 16 (2) 168-183. DOI: http://dx.doi.org/10.1080/10888705.2013.768923

McConnell, P.B. & Karen B. London (2011). *Love Has No Age Limit: Welcoming an Adopted Dog into Your Home*. Black Earth, WI. McConnell Publishing, Ltd.

Salman M.D., Jr., Janet M. Scarlett, Philip H. Kass, Rebecca Ruch-Gallie & Suzanne Hetts (1998). Human and Animal Factors Related to Relinquishment of Dogs and Cats in 12 Selected Animal Shelters in the United States, *Journal of Applied Animal Welfare Science*, 1 (3) 207-226. DOI: http://dx.doi.org/10.1207/s15327604jaws0103_2

Scarlett J.M., John G. New, Jr. & Philip H. Kass (1999). Reasons for Relinquishment of Companion Animals in U.S. Animal Shelters: Selected Health and Personal Issues, *Journal of Applied Animal Welfare Science*, 2 (1) 41-57. DOI: http://dx.doi.org/10.1207/s15327604jaws0201_4

Todd, Z. (2013). Why do people surrender dogs to animal shelters? Companion Animal Psychology blog.

About the Author

Julie Hecht is a Ph.D. student studying dog behavior and writes the Dog Spies blog at ScientificAmerican.com.

Why So Many People Have Pets

By Daisy Yuhas

O n my 10th birthday, I got a puppy. I was so shocked—I had wanted a dog for as long as I could remember—and so overwhelmed with happiness that I burst into tears. For the next 14 years, Happy, a beagle, charmed everyone he met. And when he passed, all of us who had known him mourned, as we would for any loved one. More than half of American households have a pet—that is, an animal kept primarily for companionship. And despite the fact that these housemates may bear scales, fur, fins or feathers, people often view their animals as family members. In 2014 we spent an estimated $58 billion on our animal companions and untold hours caring for them.

For 50 years psychologists have been trying to unravel the appeals of animal companionship in hopes of deciphering just why we invest so much in these creatures. In the process, anthrozoologists—scientists who study human-animal relationships—have discovered a window into human sociality more broadly. Our interactions with animals can be useful models for understanding how issues of identity, nurturing, support, and attachment play out in a relationship. "It's all about human psychology," says anthrozoologist Pauleen Bennett of La Trobe University in Australia. "Pets help us fill our need for social connectedness."

Although the motivations for pet ownership may vary as much as a golden retriever and a goldfish, scientists are finding that some common threads tie people to their household pets. Our attraction to animals may be subconscious, driven by biological and social forces that we do not fully acknowledge. In addition, the emotional bond between pets and their owners can bring varied benefits, from lowered stress to novel adventures. The more we uncover about our companion animals, the more we may learn about our human attachments as well.

Inborn Attraction?

Part of our attraction to animal companionship is innate. In 2013 psychologist Vanessa LoBue of Rutgers University and her colleagues revealed that toddlers one to three years old spend more time interacting with live animals—whether fish, hamsters, snakes, spiders, or geckos—than they do with inanimate toys when given a choice between the two.

Humans even have specialized brain cells for recognizing animal life. Researchers led by Christof Koch of the Allen Institute for Brain Science in Seattle (he also serves on *Scientific American Mind*'s board of advisers) have found neurons in the amygdala, an area involved in emotions, that respond preferentially to animal images. The 2011 finding hints at a neural basis for the powerful emotional reactions animals elicit from us.

Many animals seem to tap into humans' attraction to the adorable, a drive that also may motivate good parenting. Behavioral researchers have long noticed that humans seem to have inborn, positive responses to beings with characteristics typical of human infants—such as wide eyes, broad foreheads, and large head-to-body ratios.

To better understand the responses that cuteness can elicit, psychologist Hiroshi Nittono and his colleagues at Hiroshima University in Japan published a series of experiments in 2012 in which college students, 132 in all, searched for a digit in numerical matrices or lifted tiny objects from small holes using tweezers. Afterward, participants viewed a series of photographs before attempting the attention or motor task for a second time.

Nittono and his colleagues found that students who viewed adult animals or food—stimuli they had rated as pleasant but not cute—did not improve between trials. But the students who saw cute baby animals did the tweezer task faster and more dexterously and performed the visual search task faster the second time, suggesting that being exposed to such creatures motivates focused, attentive behavior. This finding suggests that humans are primed to attend to fragile, young infants, who may require greater care than other beings. Clearly, baby animals exploit the same instinctive responses in us that human infants elicit.

Such findings lend credence to the idea that our interest in pets stems from what biologist E. O. Wilson has called "biophilia," or an inherent tendency to focus on life and lifelike processes. Our fascination with all manner of fauna might explain why people adopt such a wide range of animal life, from tarantulas to salamanders.

Yet Wilson has also acknowledged that our interest in animals depends on personal and cultural experience. For example, dogs are popular in many Western countries but are considered unclean in traditional Islamic communities. Indeed, psychologist Harold A. Herzog of Western Carolina University has argued that pet keeping is driven principally by culture. In a paper published in 2013 Herzog and his colleagues assessed the fluctuating popularity of dog breeds using the American Kennel Club's registry from 1926 to 2005. They found no relationship between a breed's health, longevity, or behavioral traits such as aggressiveness or trainability and its popularity. Instead, they argued, the trends in top dogs were erratic and seemed to shift suddenly, as if driven by fashion. In 2014 three of the authors, including Herzog, further discovered that movies featuring specific dog breeds would boost that pooch's popularity for up to a decade. In the 10 years following the 1963 release of *The Incredible Journey*, starring a Labrador retriever, people registered Labs in the kennel club at an average rate of 2,223 dogs a year, in contrast to 452 dogs a year in the previous decade.

Extending these findings to other species, Herzog posited that people may keep pets simply because other people keep pets, reflecting our penchant for imitation. He pointed to a brief craze in the U.S. for turtle keeping, a koi fish fad in Japan, and what he jokingly identified as a brief "epidemic of Irish setters" as further evidence.

Friends with Benefits

But even if imitation plays a role in their choices, most people profess to wanting pets for companionship. This friendship then sustains the connection despite the costs of ownership. Indeed, some animal-human relationships feel similar in certain ways to human relationships. In a study published in 2014 Massachusetts General Hospital veterinarian Lori Palley and her colleagues used functional magnetic resonance imaging to measure brain activity in 14 mothers while they were looking at pictures of their children or their dogs or at pictures of other people's children or unfamiliar dogs. The researchers found that the brain activation patterns evoked by images of the women's own children and dogs were very similar and that those patterns were distinct from those elicited by unknown children and canines, suggesting that maternal feelings may extend to animals. Pets may thus help fill a human need to nurture other living beings.

An animal also can be on the flip side of this relationship, serving as a source of comfort. In the 1960s Yeshiva University child psychologist Boris Levinson observed that troubled, socially withdrawn children became talkative and enthusiastic about therapy when his dog, Jingles, was present during a session. This observation spurred a series of investigations into whether or not keeping pets could improve well-being. In a 1980 study of 92 people, biologist Erika Friedmann of the University of Pennsylvania reported that pet owners were more likely to be alive a year after a heart attack than were people who did not have a companion animal—possibly because the animals afforded some form of stress relief. Yet efforts to replicate such findings have had mixed results, and animal-assisted therapy, the field that Levinson's work inspired, has been criticized for overstating the ability of animals to ameliorate mental illness.

Nevertheless, some people may gain psychological support from their pets and keep them for exactly this reason. In a study published in 2012 psychologist Sigal Zilcha-Mano, then at the Baruch Ivcher School of Psychology at the Interdisciplinary Center Herzliya in

Israel, and her colleagues asked 285 cat or dog owners to answer a questionnaire assessing their emotional connection with their pet. Then the researchers asked 120 of these pet owners to take a challenging word test. By recording her subjects' blood pressure—a measure of stress—during the test, Zilcha-Mano found that individuals who had their pet present or thought about the pet before taking the test had lower stress than people who had no contact with the pet. Yet the strength of this benefit depended on how attached the owner was to his or her pet. In other words, the level of emotional sustenance a pet owner receives depends on how close they feel to the animal.

Different hormonal cocktails seem to underpin various degrees of animal-human attachment. In a study published in 2012 biologist Linda Handlin of the University of Skövde in Sweden and her colleagues measured levels of the bonding hormone oxytocin and stress hormone cortisol in 10 owners of female Labrador retrievers and correlated the results with self-reported data about the owners' relationships with their dogs. Owners who had higher oxytocin levels and lower cortisol levels when interacting with their dogs tended to have closer bonds with their pets. People who frequently kissed their dogs, for example, had higher levels of oxytocin, and women who reported that they dreaded their dog's death had lower cortisol levels, perhaps because they rely on their animals for stress relief.

A person's social orientation could also factor into the strength of the pet-person tie. In a study published in 2012 psychologist Andrea Beetz of the University of Rostock in Germany and her colleagues asked 47 seven- to 11-year-old boys who had difficulties forming social attachments to present a story before a committee of unfamiliar adults and then take a math test. During this ordeal, 24 of the children were accompanied by a dog, 10 had a friendly human by their side, and the others had a toy dog nearby.

Beetz found that children accompanied by a real dog had the lowest cortisol levels and that those with human company had the highest, probably because people made these boys nervous. Furthermore, among those boys who benefited from the dog, those who engaged in the most petting and other physical contact with the dog during the test showed the least stress, as measured by salivary cortisol. Thus, interacting with animals may be an especially good buffer against stress for those who find human social interaction difficult. "Some things are much easier with animals," Beetz says. "They are easier to forgive, don't talk back, and there's less inhibition when it comes to physical contact."

Animal Antics

Yet pets are much more than human substitutes. Many people with no obvious social deficits reap varied psychological benefits from owning a pet. In 2012 Bennett presented preliminary findings from a student, psychologist Jordan Schaan, then at Monash University in Australia, who had interviewed 37 dog owners who were personally and professionally successful and had an above-average connection to their animals. (The subjects were educated and affluent and had fulfilling romantic partnerships, for instance.) Among the benefits of dog ownership that these individuals reported were amusement—the animals' antics made their owners laugh—a sense of meaning from having responsibility for the welfare of another living thing, and an entrée into new experiences and relationships: a puppy can be a great way to meet neighbors.

Furthermore, many pet owners described their companion animals as instructors in a simpler, more virtuous lifestyle. Bennett and Schaan discovered that their highly successful subjects actually looked to their dogs as role models for a better life. People felt they could derive unconditional love and forgiveness from their dogs, whereas human beings seemed more likely to disappoint one another. "There's something about animals that's very genuine and honest," Bennett says. "We miss that in our human interactions."

Bennett and other anthrozoologists acknowledge that owners project some of this dynamic onto their animals. An owner can "read" a response into an animal companion's behavior regardless of the animal's intentions. Yet such projections are precisely what make this field ripe for psychology: they reveal our own social needs and desires. Animal relationships may someday provide useful comparison points to human connections—a benchmark for investigating empathy, caring, and even decision making. That these creatures can fit many molds while being so different from us makes these friendships uniquely valuable.

The study of animal companionship is still in its infancy. But without this research, we could not begin to fathom the rich and varied range of relationships that make up human experience.

Referenced

Pets in the Family: An Evolutionary Perspective. James A. Serpell and Elizabeth S. Paul in *The Oxford Handbook of Evolutionary Family Psychology*. Edited by Todd K. Shackelford and Catherine A. Salmon. Oxford University Press, 2011.

Biology, Culture, and the Origins of Pet-Keeping. Harold A. Herzog in *Animal Behavior and Cognition*, Vol. 1, No. 3, pages 269–308; August 2014.

Toward a Psychology of Human-Animal Relations. Catherine E. Amiot and Brock Bastian in *Psychological Bulletin*, Vol. 141, No. 1, pages 6–47; January 2015.

About the Author

Daisy Yuhas is an associate editor at Scientific American Mind.

Good (and Bad) Ways to Help
a Dog Afraid of Fireworks

By Julie Hecht

First, let's get the bad out of the way: trying to help a dog afraid of fireworks by saying, "Johnny (that's the dog) there will be fireworks tomorrow night. Don't you go running away at the park like you did last year! That was bad, Johnny. Very bad. So this year, get ahold of yourself!"

Unfortunately, monologues like this won't make Johnny any more comfortable with this year's fireworks. Nor will scolding—or in any way punishing—alter Johnny's behavior for the better or help him push through this difficult situation. And bringing Johnny to fireworks is like putting someone wearing an itty bitty bathing suit outside on a scorching summer day without a drop of sunscreen and saying, "Don't get sunburned, love!" When it comes to loud noises or sun, avoid this formula: Zero Protection + Massive Exposure = Very Bad Outcome.

OK, don't bring Johnny to the park for the loud explosions, check. But what then? How can we help Johnny? While there is not a one-size-fits-all solution, a number of studies point out what to consider when a dog's not a fan of fireworks.

Hear No Evil

Try to insulate dogs from the booms outside. This means no backyards and maybe not even free run of the house. Instead, keep the dog in a safe, enclosed area where they cannot hurt themselves if panicked. Think internal quiet zone away from outside walls and windows. In Portland, Oregon at Synergy Behavior Solutions, Valli Parthasarathy—a veterinarian on her way to becoming a board-certified veterinary behavior specialist—hosts a Fourth of July Hideaway for dogs and their people. A quiet, safe space plus a movie! In your home, background noise like TV, fans, or white noise can help mask what's going on outside.

In It Together

Does this sound familiar? "You'll make it worse by trying to comfort Johnny. Ignoring him is your best bet." If a power-through-it approach speaks to you, consider reconsidering. A number of studies highlight that dogs value social support from owners. Like a child afraid of a loud noise turning and running toward a parent, dogs facing stressful situations have been found to turn to their owners as safe havens.

In a 2013 open access study, Márta Gácsi and colleagues found that when encountering a threatening stranger, the increase in dog heart rate was less pronounced when the dog's owner was present than when the dog encountered the threatening stranger alone. The researchers' conclusion: "similar to parents of infants, owners can provide a buffer against stress in dogs..." Being there for your dog can help.

What you do while there can also help. Studies from Isabella Merola and colleagues found that the emotions we display can affect how dogs respond to potentially scary things. In their 2012 studies, one of which is open access, dogs encountered an unfamiliar, strange object that could elicit a mild fear response—an electric fan with plastic green ribbons streaming from it. When encountering the Crazy Green Monster (that's what I call it), the researchers wanted to know whether dog behavior—their approach to or avoidance of the Monster—was affected by owner behavior—whether the owner behaved in a happy or fearful manner. What owners did mattered. Dogs were more likely to approach the weird object if owners spoke in a happy voice and smiled, seeming to convey, "It's all good."

While fireworks—unpredictable and intensely loud noises accompanied by flashes of light—are not necessarily equivalent to a threatening stranger or a weird blowing object, these studies highlight that people can serve as a support for their dogs.

Veterinary behaviorist Melissa Bain comments in a *New York Times* interview, "You can't reinforce anxiety by comforting a dog....You won't make the fear worse. Do what you need to do to help your dog."

At the same time, it's not about forcing a dog to get comfort from you. If a dog seeks you out, that's one thing. If not, don't push it. Comfort is not achieved through force, and there are many other ways to turn a dog's frown upside down.

What Fireworks?

What decreases one dog's fear may not work for the next, which is why we have reserves! One study found anxiety wraps to be useful for some dogs. Adaptil, a "synthetic pheromone that mimics the pheromone mother dogs emit after giving birth to help their puppies," has also been found to decrease signs of fear in dogs fearful of fireworks.

Tasty, tasty food is an incredible resource because it can help change a dog's emotional state and thereby change the dog's outward behavior. Veterinary behaviorist Ilana Reisner gives this great recommendation: "Before the fireworks start, cook up an irresistible food such as chicken breast, special meat, or salmon cookies, microwave tiny bits of nitrate-free hot dogs, popcorn. Stock a treat bag. Feed one piece at a time to your dog throughout the fireworks to countercondition and distract. If your dog is willing, make a game of it and ask her sit, down, 'find it', shake hands and other distracting cues. Freeze a Kong with kibble mixed with baby food. Feed dinner through the toy."

A drug approved last May by the FDA for canine noise aversion is also promising. Sileo inhibits the development of fear and anxiety by blocking norepinephrine release, which provides a calming effect without sedation. This drastically contrasts with another drug, acepromazine (Ace for short), which is not recommended. It acts as a tranquilizer and does not alleviate fear or anxiety. "What it does do though, and do well, is make them unable to move and/or exhibit any of the other outward signs of their fear and anxiety. Ace is kind of like a 'chemical straightjacket' in these instances," explains Jason Nicholas of Preventive Vet. Sounds like the perfect nightmare. Medications should always be discussed with a veterinarian.

Dogs don't mix well with celebratory booms in the sky, but the good news is they don't have to go it alone. How do you plan to help your dog through the bangs and the booms?

The views expressed are those of the author(s) and are not necessarily those of Scientific American.

Referenced

Cottam N, Dodman NH, Ha JC (2012) The effectiveness of the Anxiety Wrap in the treatment of canine thunderstorm phobia: An open-label trial. *Journal of Veterinary Behavior: Clinical Applications and Research* 8, 154-161.

Gácsi M, Maros K, Sernkvist S, Faragó T, Miklósi Á (2013) Human Analogue Safe Haven Effect of the Owner: Behavioural and Heart Rate Response to Stressful Social Stimuli in Dogs. *PLoS ONE* 8(3): e58475

Merola I, Prato-Previde E, Marshall-Pescini S (2012) Social referencing in dog-owner dyads? *Animal Cognition* 15, 175-185.

Merola I, Prato-Previde E, Marshall-Pescini S (2012) Dogs' Social Referencing towards Owners and Strangers. *PLoS ONE* 7(10): e47653.

About the Author

Julie Hecht is a Ph.D. student studying dog behavior and writes the Dog Spies blog at ScientificAmerican.com.

Culture Shapes How Children View the Natural World

By Jason G. Goldman

How do young children understand the natural world? Most research into this question has focused on urban, white, middle-class American children living near large universities. Even when psychologists include kids from other communities, too often they use experimental procedures originally developed for urban children. Now researchers have developed a methodology for studying rural Native American kids' perspectives on nature and have compared their responses with those of their city-dwelling peers. The findings offer some rare cross-cultural insight into early childhood environmental education.

Sandra Waxman, a developmental psychologist at Northwestern University, and her colleagues have long collaborated with the Menominee, a Native American nation in Wisconsin. When the researchers presented plans for their study to tribe members who were trained research assistants, the assistants protested that the experiment—which involved watching children play with toy animals—was not culturally appropriate. It does not make sense to the Menominee to think of animals as divorced from their ecological contexts, Waxman says.

Instead one of the Menominee researchers constructed a diorama that included realistic trees, grass, and rocks, as well as the original toy animals. The researchers watched as three groups of four-year-olds played with the diorama: rural Menominee, as well as Native Americans and other Americans living in Chicago and its suburbs.

All three groups were more likely to enact realistic scenarios with the toy animals than imaginary scenarios. But both groups of Native American kids were more likely to imagine they were the animals rather than give the animals human attributes. And the rural Menominee were especially talkative during the experiment, contrary to previous research that characterized these children as less verbal than their non–Native American peers. The results were published last November in the *Journal of Cognition and Development*.

"The involvement of tribal communities in all aspects of the research—planning, design, execution, analysis and dissemination—has to be the minimum requirement of all research involving Native people," says Iowa State University STEM scholars program director Corey Welch, who is a member of the Northern Cheyenne.

About the Author

Jason G. Goldman is a science journalist based in Los Angeles. He has written about animal behavior, wildlife biology, conservation, and ecology for Scientific American, Los Angeles *magazine, the* Washington Post, *the* Guardian, *the BBC,* Conservation *magazine, and elsewhere. He contributes to* Scientific American's *"60-Second Science" podcast, and is co-editor of* Science Blogging: The Essential Guide *(Yale University Press). He enjoys sharing his wildlife knowledge on television and on the radio, and often speaks to the public about wildlife and science communication.*

People with COVID Often Infect Their Pets

By Frank Schubert

D ogs or cats that live in a household with people who have COVID often become infected and sick themselves. Experts advise infected individuals to keep a distance from their animals if possible.

New research shows that people who become infected with the novel coronavirus, or SARS-CoV-2, and fall ill often pass the pathogen on to their pets. The animals sometimes also become sick from the infection, occasionally severely, according to the results of two separate studies presented at this year's European Congress of Clinical Microbiology and Infectious Diseases. The papers have not yet been published in scientific journals.

A team led by veterinarian Dorothee Bienzle of the University of Guelph in Ontario investigated potential COVID infection in 198 cats and 54 dogs. All of the dogs and 48 of the cats came from a household in which at least one person had COVID, and the rest of the cats came from an animal shelter or neuter clinic. The team found that two out of three cats and two out of five dogs whose owners had COVID had antibodies against SARS-CoV-2, indicating they had been infected with the virus at some point, too But in the shelter group, less than one in 10 cats had these antibodies. And in the neuter clinic, the figure was less than one in 38.

Dogs and cats that came from households in which owners had COVID also often developed symptoms of the disease, Bienzle and her team report. Between 20 and 30 percent of the animals experienced loss of energy and appetite, coughing, diarrhea, runny nose, and respiratory problems. The complications were mostly mild and short-term, but they were severe in three cases. In cats, the risk of infection was higher in those that were closely cuddled by their owners, according to behavioral surveys the researchers conducted in addition to the antibody tests. This cuddling correlation was not observed in dogs.

Veterinarian Els Broens of Utrecht University in the Netherlands and her colleagues conducted similar studies on 156 dogs and 154 cats from about 200 households with human COVID patients. The researchers found that animals in one in five of these households had become infected with the virus—results identified by positive polymerase chain reaction (PCR) or antibody tests. Disease symptoms, especially respiratory and gastrointestinal complications, also occurred in the animals but were mostly mild.

Both Bienzle's and Broens's groups conclude that humans often transmit SARS-CoV-2 to their pets. "This is not at all surprising," says Sarah Hamer, a veterinary epidemiologist at Texas A&M University, who is conducting similar studies on COVID-positive pets in the U.S. As research rolls in, she says, the international veterinary field is finding that pet owners transmitting the virus to their furry friends is more common than originally thought. "The findings are consistent: it's just not that hard for these animals to get infected," Hamer says. That result makes sense, she explains, given the closeness of person-pet relationships. "Often we're snuggling and even sleeping in the same beds with them," Hamer says.

The role pets and livestock play in the COVID pandemic has been debated for some time. Several studies have shown that pigs, cows, ducks, and chickens seem to be largely resistant to the virus. Cats frequently become infected at higher rates than dogs, Hamer notes, and pass the pathogen on to fellow felines. Beyond the pathogen posing a risk to our pets' health, researchers worry that it will multiply in the animals and possibly mutate, jumping back into humans at some point. "The main concern is ... the potential risk that pets could act as a reservoir of the virus and reintroduce it into the human population," Broens says. Mink have been shown to retransmit SARS-CoV-2 to humans, leading some countries to take drastic measures to prevent the pathogen from spreading on mink farms. Denmark and the Netherlands culled their mink stocks, killing almost 20 million of the furry animals in total to stop the virus from spreading further.

So far, Broens says, there is no evidence of such retransmission from dogs and cats back into humans. But Hamer notes the current studies simply are not set up to answer that exact question. In the meantime, the researchers recommend pet owners exercise caution. "If you have COVID-19, my advice is to keep your distance from your pet and don't let them into your bedroom," Bienzle says. Hamer reiterates that the recommendations are the same as with any other humans in your household: if you're infected, stay as far away as possible.

This article originally appeared in Spektrum der Wissenschaft *and was reproduced with permission with additional reporting by Tess Joosse.*

Most Pets Can't Sweat: Here's What You Can Do for Them in a Heat Wave

By Stella Marie Hombach

P anting, increased grooming, a dip in the lake. All of these measures are what pets use to cope with a prolonged heat spell. Animals have evolved their own methods to cool off. In the wild, all of this works well. Pets, however, depend on the help of their owners to gain access to these relief measures. Such concerns are highlighted by increasingly frequent heat waves, such as the one that has seen temperatures in Sacramento, Calif., climb above 110 degrees Fahrenheit (43 degrees Celsius) in early September—and the blistering July temperatures that beset places as far afield as the United Kingdom and China.

Veterinarian Michael Leschnik from the University Clinic for Small Animals in Vienna, Austria, explains here what dogs, rabbits, and the like need when exposed to intense heat.

[An edited transcript of the interview follows.]

Q: At temperatures of up to 37 degrees C (99 degrees F), we humans work up quite a sweat, and for some this is very stressful. How do pets cope?
A: Heat is also exhausting for them. Unlike us, however, most of them can't sweat.

Q: Why is sweating important when it's warm?
A: When we sweat, the heart pumps more blood through the body, the blood vessels and pores of the skin dilate, and the sweat produced by the sweat glands comes out. When it evaporates, it helps us maintain a constant core body temperature. Dogs and cats also have sweat glands on the balls of their feet, but these are not sufficient. Pigs and rabbits, on the other hand, have no ability to sweat at all.

118

Q: What strategies do animals use instead?

A: They vary. Many pant, first and foremost. The rapid breathing motion causes the throat to produce saliva, and the evaporation cools. The body also releases heat via exhalation and the nasal secretions produced by panting. This is particularly visible in dogs, but birds and cats can also pant. But this breathing technique is strenuous and causes the animals to expend more energy.

Q: So panting regulates the internal body temperature only for a short time?

A: Other methods are needed. Cats, for example, increasingly lick their fur. This makes it damp and the evaporation brings cooling. Most animals also like to take a bath, look for a place in the shade, shift physical activities to the morning and evening hours, and drink more than usual. Basically the same strategies as for us humans.

Q: Why is rest so important for us and animals?

A: Exercise causes the body to produce heat. To avoid overheating, the body then has to dissipate it, and that costs energy. Most animals therefore instinctively retreat in the heat. Only dogs don't find this so easy.

Q: What distinguishes dogs from other animals in this respect?

A: Their close relationship with humans. Strong domestication has deprived them of many of their instincts. If I go jogging with my dog in 37-degree-C weather or let the animal run alongside my bicycle, he'll go along with it. This is because dogs are designed to follow their owner or owner's lead. This is why there are always dogs that collapse even though there is a lake nearby.

Q: Does this have to do with their domestication?

A: The animals I'm talking about don't chill in the shade or splash in the water, but are kept busy by their mistress or master for hours retrieving a Frisbee. A few jumps into the water no longer compensate for the heat that their bodies produce through the movement and high temperatures. Neither the dogs nor their owners realize that they need a break. With cats it's different: they are no longer lions, but they have largely retained their instincts; it's difficult to motivate them to play in the blazing sun. The same applies to rodents or birds.

Q: Speaking of which, what about guinea pigs, mice, and rabbits? How do they deal with heat?

A: They too, need rest, shade and plenty of fluids. Instead of panting, some of them also use their ears. These are equipped with a network of fine blood vessels. In hot temperatures, the vessels dilate and thus dissipate heat. Unlike dogs and cats, rodents are often kept in cages or outdoor enclosures. If this occurs during the day directly in the sun without recourse to a shady retreat, cooling over the ears or increased drinking is not enough. Then these animals are also in danger of overheating. The same applies to birds and fish. It helps to cover parts of enclosures or aquariums with a cloth.

Q: So anyone who keeps a pet should make sure that cages are in the shade?

A: And keep in mind the course of the sun. After all, it moves throughout the day, changing the intensity of the sun's rays. Sometimes it helps to cover parts of the animals' enclosures or aquariums with a cloth. In addition, with fish, the water must always be controlled: If the temperature rises too much, it is important to add cool water. This is because the heat also reduces the oxygen content. This triggers stress, and in extreme cases the animals lack the oxygen they need to breathe.

Q: Does it also depend on the breed whether the heat is difficult for a dog or cat?

A: Pugs, bulldogs, and Persian cats have a particularly hard time. Through breeding, their skulls, especially the nose and upper jaw, have been shortened more and more. Adult animals keep their childlike snub nose. The result is narrowed nostrils and nasal cavities, a lengthened and thickened soft palate, and changes in the larynx, which lead to breathing problems in many. This makes it difficult for animals to regulate their body temperature by panting. Increased risk also exists for pets that are quite old, have diseases such as diabetes or heart problems, or are overweight. This is because subcutaneous fat cannot conduct heat well, making thermoregulation more difficult. Overall, there is basically no difference from what happens to us humans.

Q: What about animals that have a lot of fur, like longhaired cats? Do they suffer more than others?

A: Not necessarily. Due to the air circulation between skin and fur, longer hair sometimes even has a cooling effect. In addition, the hair protects against sunburn. However, it can be helpful to regularly remove the undercoat, the hair that lies closer to the body, by brushing.

Q: What else can you do to help pets through hot summers?

A: Walk your dog in the cool morning and evening hours. The same goes for dog training sessions. Similar to birds, dogs also enjoy a bathing opportunity, and some like to be gently showered with lukewarm water from a spray bottle. Rodents can be given a second water bottle to hang in their cage and offered more fresh green food. There is additional water in lettuce, cucumber, and peppers. Animals that are fed wet food, such as cats, should be offered small portions, as this food spoils quickly in the heat. It's also very important not to leave animals in the car when it is hot, which unfortunately happens again and again.

In the blazing sun, temperatures in the car quickly rise to more than 70 degrees C (158 degrees F). A window opened ajar and a small bowl of water are then no longer sufficient for thermoregulation, nor is panting. Animals, usually dogs, can thus quickly get heatstroke.

Q: What exactly happens during heatstroke?

A: Due to the rising body temperature, an animal's metabolism is stimulated more and more and becomes increasingly overloaded. From a body temperature of 42 degrees C (108 degrees F), vital proteins are also destroyed and the metabolism ultimately breaks down. This leads to multiple organ failures, which in many cases can occur only after one or two days.

Q: What can owners do in case of heatstroke?

A: Common symptoms are increased salivation, balance disorders, vomiting, diarrhea, and even unconsciousness. When these occur, they need to bring the animal into the shade, offer it water, and cool it with cold towels. Often the animal also needs a vet, sometimes even a stay in the hospital. These first aid measures should be familiar to everyone who has an animal.

Q: Is there any other tip you would like to give to people with animals?

A: Think about what is good for you in the heat. Maybe that will also suit your dog or your budgie. Because when it comes to dealing with heat, most animals are more like us than we think. If you're not sure, ask your veterinarian.

About the Author

Stella Marie Hombach works as a freelance journalist and systemic consultant in Berlin. You can find more information on her website: stellahombach.de.

Section 5: Other Pets in Our Lives

What is the Difference Between Hair and Fur?

By Kate Wong

Scientific American writer Kate Wong spoke with mammalogist Nancy Simmons of the American Museum of Natural History in New York City about this question. An edited transcript of the interview follows.

SA: Is there a difference between hair and fur?

NS: There isnt. Hair and fur are the same thing.

SA: Why is it then that, for example, my dogs fur is three inches long and it never seems to grow longer, while my own hair keeps growing and growing?

NS: Actually, a lot of types of human hair won't keep growing and growing. The normal length of the hair is an individual and species specific trait. So across the breadth of mammals, there are many norms for hair length, or fur length.

What's really different is the pattern of where it grows. Your dog or cat is basically covered with hair, whereas humans tend to grow hair in a few selected places. And thats one of the things that have changed through evolution in a number of mammal groups. Whales, for instance, are mammals, but they are nearly hairless. We lack hair over a lot of our bodies.

SA: Is hair a defining characteristic of mammals?

NS: It's one of them. Other features that define mammals include producing milk to nourish the offspring.

SA: When does hair appear to have arisen?

NS: We dont know, because the evolutionary lineage leading to mammals includes many fossil forms going way back in time, and hair, as a rule, doesnt fossilize. So we cant know whether many of these relatives of mammals from the age of dinosaurs and earlier had hair or not.

SA: Are there any impressions of hair in the fossil record?

NS: There are very few fossils where there are impressions of anything in terms of soft tissue.

SA: How did hair evolve?

NS: I think most evolutionary biologists believe that the evolution of hair is correlated with the evolution of endothermy, or warm-bloodedness, the ability to produce internal body heatand hair is a very good insulator. If youre going to spend a lot of metabolic energy heating your body, its more efficient to hold on to that heat and not to lose it to the environment around you. So having hair as a means of insulation is one of the ideas about why we have hair. Of course, there is no way for us to tell whether hair evolved first and then endothermy evolved, or whether endothermy evolved and then somehow hair evolved. We really dont know anything about these things.

SA: Humans evolved in Africa, along with a lot of primates that are covered with fur. Why did humans lose most of theirs?

NS: We don't know. Theres a lot of variation in how much of the body is covered with fur in various primate groups. Some are incredibly hairy, and some have considerably less fur on the face and the chest and so on. Primates tend to rely on facial expressions for social communication, and of course the better you can see the face, perhaps the better that social communication works. That doesnt mean you have to get rid of the hair to see the face. That just happens to be what happened in apes. But that could be one of the reasons why we dont have hair on our faces.

SA: Is a whisker a special kind of hair?

NS: Yes, it is. There are many different kinds of modified hairs to which we give different names. A porcupines quills are greatly enlarged hairs. Whiskers are hairs that work as sensory receptors. There's a strange animal from the Old World called a pangolin, which has these scaly plates that cover most of its body. Those are modified hairs.

SA: So this is all the same material?

NS: This is all the same material.

SA: How does a whisker work as a sensory receptor?

NS: It has to do with its size, and whiskers have special nervous connections that make them highly sensitive to movement. Those nerves are directly connected to a part of the brain that keeps track of that information and allows the animal to interpret it as sensory information in conjunction with the other information its getting from adjacent whiskers.

SA: When you see something that looks like a whisker on a catfish, for example, what is that structure?

NS: Well, its a similar structure in the sense that it is a long, skinny thing that sticks out from the body and is used to help sense whats going on in the environment. But its not homologous; its independently evolved. Its not made of the same material, and it wasnt inherited from a common ancestor. Its a completely different structure that may serve something of the same purpose, but completely independently.

We may think about human hair—curly versus straight versus whatever—as being really different from what animals have, but if you think of the breadth of mammals out there you can find equivalents in many other groups for long hair versus short hair versus tightly curled hair and all that. You can actually find all of that in dogs, without even having to look to other species.

Ferrets: Man's Other Best Friend

By Jason G. Goldman

If a human points their finger at something, a dog might infer that there's hidden food, while the chimpanzee remains more or less clueless about the meaning behind that sort of non-verbal communication. As dogs have evolved in a social space occupied by human social partners, they've gained the unique ability not only to comprehend human social-communicative cues, but perhaps even to manipulate humans, and certainly to initiate communicative interactions with humans.

One study found that dogs are more likely to ask a human for food if the human's eyes are visible, suggesting that dogs understanding something about human attention. (They also might be more likely to try to eat from a "forbidden" bowl if a human's eyes are closed.) Unlike wolves, dogs make eye contact with humans in an effort to receive help in solving an "impossible" task. All of this is to say that dogs are suited to socializing with humans in a way that even the other great apes—species more genetically related to humans—are not.

One might suppose that dogs' impressive social cognitive skills arise from experience interacting with humans rather than from genetics, but experiments with human-raised wolves as well as with domesticated goats, horses, cats, and foxes all point towards domestication—that is, genetics—as the root of many of these abilities. If domestication lies at the heart of these sorts of social-cognitive skills, then domestic ferrets should share some of the same social cognitive skills, particularly when it comes to comprehending human social cues, as the others in the domestic menagerie.

Ferrets are a carnivorous species that have not yet been rigorously studied when it comes to social cognition, or really at all within the field of psychology. "Although their early history in service of man is obscure," write Hungarian researchers Anna Hernad, Anna Kis, Borbala Turcsan, and Jozsef Topal last week in a new paper in PLoS ONE, "ferrets have probably been domesticated for more than two thousand years by selective breeding from the European polecat (*Mustela putorious*)." Like dogs, they say, ferrets originally were bred for practical reasons like hunting. Their role within human society has since shifted, as they now predominantly serve as pets. If ferrets adapted to a new social ecology within human society as have other domestic species, like dogs and horses, then they ought to respond to humans differently than their wild forebears.

Seventeen domestic ferrets were compared in three experiments to 16 human-raised wild mustelids and 18 domestic dogs. (Mustelids include polecats, weasels, otters, badgers, minks, and others. The wild mustelids in this study were hybrids of those species.) Importantly, all the wild mustelids were raised by humans and kept as pets. Any differences in their behavior would therefore be attributable to domestication rather than to being raised by humans.

First, the three groups of animals were compared for their tolerance for eye-contact. The domestic species—ferrets and dogs—tolerated prolonged eye-contact from their owners, but not from strangers, while the wild mustelids did not show this distinction. Ferrets and dogs were also both more likely to accept food from their owners than from strangers, while the wild mustelids made their approach decisions randomly, equally preferring their owners and a stranger (In fact, there was a slight but statistically insignificant preference for the stranger!) In both experiments, domestic ferrets' performance was significantly different from the wild mustelids, but not statistically distinguishable from the responses of the domestic dogs. Rather than sorting along genetic lines, performance in these tasks could be explained by domestication.

The third experiment tested each group's response to two types of pointing: *momentary pointing*, in which an unfamiliar experimenter briefly pointed at one of two containers that could have contained food, but did not make physical contact with it, and *sustained touching*, in which the experimented physically touched one of the two containers.

In both conditions, as in the other experiments, ferrets and dogs preferred eating from the container that the experimenter had indicated, while the wild mustelids did not display a preference for either container. And, as before, the ferrets' performance was statistically different from the wild mustelids', but not from the dogs' responses.

It is telling that of the 16 wild mustelid hybrids, a large proportion of them would not even participate in the third experiment; they completely ignored the experimenter. Those that did participate, however, were more likely to have a domestic ferret in their recent ancestry.

The researchers conclude that the domestic ferrets' social-cognitive skills are a result of domestication, and are therefore related to genetic differences between domestic ferrets and their wild cousins, rather than differences in experience. This lends further support to the "syndrome" hypothesis of domestication, which holds that selection for one trait (such as tameness, or tolerance for humans in close proximity) can result in a wide variety of correlated byproducts that also emerge as a result of that selection, including behavioral and cognitive traits as well as anatomical and physiological ones. "The fact that domestic ferrets seem to be more 'dog-like' than 'wild ferret-like' regarding their social-affiliative behaviors and responsiveness to human [gestures]," they write, "strongly supports the notion that (at least some of the) domestic species have acquired a set of social skills that improve their chances to survive in human communities."

The views expressed are those of the author(s) and are not necessarily those of Scientific American.

Referenced

Hernádi A, Kis A, Turcsán B, & Topál J (2012). Man's Underground Best Friend: Domestic Ferrets, Unlike the Wild Forms, Show Evidence of Dog-Like Social-Cognitive Skills. *PloS one*, 7 (8) PMID: 22905244

About the Author

Jason G. Goldman is a science journalist based in Los Angeles. He has written about animal behavior, wildlife biology, conservation, and ecology for Scientific

American, Los Angeles *magazine, the* Washington Post, *the* Guardian, *the BBC,* Conservation *magazine, and elsewhere. He contributes to* Scientific American's *"60-Second Science" podcast, and is co-editor of* Science Blogging: The Essential Guide *(Yale University Press). He enjoys sharing his wildlife knowledge on television and on the radio, and often speaks to the public about wildlife and science communication.*

Our Love of Exotic Pets Is Driving Wildlife Decline

By Richard Conniff

Conservation biologist David S. Wilcove was on a birding trip to the Indonesian island of Sumatra in 2012, when he began to notice that house after house in every village he visited had cages hanging outside, inhabited by the kinds of wild birds he had expected to see in the forest. One in five households in Indonesia keeps birds as pets. That got him thinking, "What is this doing to the birds?"

To find out, Wilcove, who teaches at Princeton University, made a detour from his planned itinerary to visit the Pramuka bird market in the capital city of Jakarta, Southeast Asia's largest market for birds and other wildlife, from bats to monkeys. "It was this sort of Walmart-size space filled with hundreds of stalls," each of which was filled with hundreds of birds, he recalls. "An awful lot of them were in very poor condition, with signs of disease, feathers frayed, behaving listlessly—or thrashing around in their cages because a lot of these are wild birds that are not at all suited to living as caged birds." Some were species that even zoos with highly trained professional staff cannot maintain in captivity; they would die soon after purchase, "the cut-flower syndrome," Wilcove remarks. "It was really a shocking sight. I've never seen anything like it."

Research by Wilcove and his colleagues subsequently linked demand for birds in Indonesia's pet marketplace to the decline of numerous species in the wild. Prices in the pet market, they suggested in a 2015 study in *Biological Conservation*, can even serve as an alarm system for species declines that might not show up in field studies until years later, if at all: when the average price for a white-rumped shama, a popular species in Indonesian songbird competitions, shot up by 1,500 percent from 2013 to 2015, the shift tipped off conservationists that these birds were vanishing from the wild.

131

Follow-up field studies in Indonesia by Bert Harris, a co-author of the 2015 study now at the Virginia-based Rainforest Trust, found no trace of white-rumped shamas, even in seemingly intact habitats where they should thrive, such as forests five kilometers from the nearest roads. Buyers were paying especially high prices for vulnerable island populations of the birds, many of them now recognized as separate species but valued by collectors for novel features such as long tails or distinctive songs. The pet trade has "the potential to drive species to extinction even when they have suitable habitat," Wilcove observes, "and to do so without anyone being aware of it."

The problem is not just about birds. Nor is it limited to Indonesia or other developing nations. The trade in wild-caught pets is driven at least as much by demand from collectors in the U.S. and Europe. Aquariums in the U.S., for example, are the final destination for about 11 million fish, along with other marine creatures, plucked from coral reefs every year, by some estimates. American pet dealers annually import 225 million live animals on average. They brought in more than 3 billion over the first 14 years of this century, according to a recent study in *EcoHealth*. Despite the widespread belief that our love of pets is one of the finer aspects of human nature, researchers increasingly suggest that it has become a major force in what they call defaunation, the great vanishing of wildlife from habitats of all kinds, almost everywhere.

Beyond Habitat Loss

For decades conservationists emphasized the role of ecosystem destruction in driving biodiversity decline. But the booming trade in wild animals, with more species taken to meet international demand for pets than for any other purpose, has caused increasing alarm. "The idea that habitat loss is the greatest threat to species survival is starting to be questioned," says Crawford Allan of the wildlife trade-monitoring network TRAFFIC, a collaboration between the WWF and the International Union for Conservation of Nature

(IUCN). "There are certain species that have plenty of habitat; however, they are being sucked up from the wild at alarming rates."

Consumer demand for rare species has made the pet trade a source of special concern among conservationists. The IUCN Red List of Threatened Species already includes many species pushed to the brink by trapping for the pet trade, among them birds (the Bali myna and South America's Spix's macaw), a primate (Southeast Asia's greater slow loris), ornamental fishes (Asia's red line torpedo barb), and reptiles (Madagascar's radiated and ploughshare tortoises). And these are just the well-studied species, according to Wilcove and Harris. For the vast majority of vertebrates sold in markets and pet stores, researchers have not even begun to assess how the pet trade affects wild populations.

Field studies to answer such questions inevitably progress slowly, but the market for pets can move with devastating and unpredictable speed. In one notorious case from the 1990s, researchers published the first scientific description of the Roti Island snake-necked turtle, including the standard details about where it lives—an island in southern Indonesia. Collectors pounced, and the species is now critically endangered. Having learned this painful lesson, biologists withheld precise location information in 2011, when they described the new Matilda's horned viper from the highlands of southern Tanzania. Dealers nonetheless had the snakes on the market that same year at more than $500 apiece, according to a 2016 study of the European reptile trade published in *Biological Conservation*.

Dealers and collectors justify the sale of wild-caught animals as pets under the guise of conservation, observes a reptile trade investigator who asked not to be named: "They say, 'We are maintaining insurance populations.' Or, 'The wild habitat is being destroyed, so we are protecting these animals.' In the vast majority of cases, that's not true." Rather, the investigator asserts, the pet trade itself is decimating wild populations.

For instance, the critically endangered ploughshare tortoise, a handsome species with a domed, golden shell, lives only in Baly Bay National Park in northwestern Madagascar. Commercial exploitation has been banned since 1975 under the Convention on International Trade in Endangered Species of Wild Fauna and Flora (CITES), and conservationists worked for decades to rebuild the population in the wild to an estimated 600 to 800 individuals. But over the past five years a surge in poaching to supply collectors has reduced the ploughshare population at Baly Bay to fewer than 100 adults. In countries such as Thailand, Indonesia, and China, which tend to honor CITES rules on paper but not in practice, speculators have driven the price for a large ploughshare adult up to $100,000.

Financial speculation was also the apparent motivation in 2015, when a Chinese businessman paid more than $200,000 for a red-necked pond turtle, a species from southern China now thought to be extinct in the wild. "The more rare species get, the closer to extinction, the more these dealers promote that as a sales thing, and the higher the prices become," says Rick Hudson, a herpetologist and president of the Texas-based nonprofit Turtle Survival Alliance.

The same players who supply the trade in wild animal parts—from rhinoceros horn to crocodile skin—are also fueling the pet trade. "Many of these people who were doing the traditional medicine trade are now branching out because the high-end pet trade in China has grown immensely" and has escalated prices in Europe and the U.S., says Brian Horne, a herpetologist for the Wildlife Conservation Society. Criminal elements have also gotten involved, at times targeting the captive breeding facilities set up by conservationists to rebuild populations of imperiled species. Thieves broke into one such facility last year in Thailand and stole six ploughshares and 72 radiated tortoises. They also target collectors. In Hong Kong last year, for instance, robbers broke into a family's home, scaling drainpipes and bypassing security cameras to steal 23 endangered turtles worth an estimated $116,000.

Catching and prosecuting people who traffic in illegal wildlife is one obvious way to slow the emptying of natural habitats. In 2016 a judge sentenced a Pennsylvania man to two years in prison in a scheme to export North American wood turtles, a threatened species. According to federal investigators, John Tokosh, then age

54, collected 750 of them from a small area south of Pittsburgh, immobilized them with duct tape for shipping and sold them at $400 apiece to middlemen supplying the pet trade in Hong Kong. That case also led to jail terms for a postal worker in Louisiana and collaborators in Chicago and California.

But such prosecutions are relatively rare. The enormous scale of the pet trade, both into and out of the country, inevitably overwhelms port inspectors working to spot contraband. "We do a lot of these blitzes, we call them, and it's such an absolute needle in a haystack," says one U.S. Fish and Wildlife Service inspector who asked to not be named because he was not authorized to speak to the press. "We have all the tools. We've gotten more equipment and more people. We have a great intelligence unit. It just seems like we're always behind the eight ball. By the time we figure it out, everything has changed." In one case, a dealer smuggled an orangutan into the country by trimming its hair, dyeing it brown and mixing it into a legal shipment of another primate.

The sheer variety of species being traded also reduces the likelihood of detection. "There's nobody out there who knows all the birds," says Eric Goode, founder of the nonprofit Turtle Conservancy, based in New York City. "Tropical fish, unless you get the world's top ichthyologist, they don't know how to identify all those species. In the case of turtles [and tortoises], there are only 340 species on the planet," but inspectors typically "can't tell a Burmese star tortoise from an Indian star tortoise or one soft-shelled turtle from another." CITES may ban all trade in a critically endangered turtle or parrot, he adds, but traffickers "just label it as a more common variety" and go on about their business.

Catch or Breed?

Goode and others argue that if the pet trade cares about conservation, suppliers should stop harvesting animals from the wild and focus on breeding them in captivity. "There's a point when you have to walk the walk," he says. "Let's really stop the importation of wildlife, stop the importation of wild birds, stop the Russian tortoises," a species from Central Asia commonly sold in U.S. pet stores. "Go to any of these warehouses and see the staggering mortality that occurs every day. Why do you need this constant flow of animals into the U.S. that are caught in the wild?"

Captive breeding could be the answer to the bird trade in Indonesia, where many households already keep captive-bred lovebirds, Wilcove says. A program aimed at increasing availability of inexpensive budgerigars, canaries, and other pet-friendly species might help persuade people that they do not "need to own a shama or to buy some of these wild-caught birds that are not suited to living in a cage." As a child, he adds, he used a recording by "the Pavarotti of the canary world" to train his pet canary to sing. "There's no reason canaries couldn't become fierce competitors" in Indonesian singing competitions, Wilcove observes.

But captive breeding can also be harder than it might seem. In 2014 EcoHealth Alliance, a New York City–based nonprofit, established its EcoHealthy Pets Web site, modeled on the Monterey Bay Aquarium's Seafood Watch, to alert consumers to the best and worst choices in exotic pets. The list emphasizes captive breeding as a way to reduce both health risks and pressure on the natural world. But lack of financial support to expand this program has so far limited the list to just 52 species, not nearly enough to satisfy even many beginning hobbyists.

The pet industry has remained ambivalent about a broad commitment to captive breeding, in part because no one has figured out how to breed many animal groups that are popular as pets. And when they do figure it out, they may find that raising an animal to maturity is far more expensive than simply catching it from the wild. When breeders in the lucrative saltwater aquarium fish trade learned how to rear colorful mandarinfish, for instance, "the mass market didn't want to pay $40 for a captive-bred fish they could get for $12 from wild-caught sources," Scott Fellman, an aquarium trade retailer, complained in an online forum. "Shame on us, as a hobby, for not doing more to support efforts like this," he added.

Further complicating matters, many self-styled captive-breeding facilities also replenish their stock from the wild and may thus serve merely to launder the wholesale removal of wildlife from habitats. For instance, the number of purportedly captive-bred Papuan hornbills being exported "far exceeds what breeding facilities can hold or yield, given the species' slow reproductive rate," conservation geneticist Laura Tensen of the University of Johannesburg reported in a survey of wildlife farming published in 2016 in *Global Ecology and Conservation*. Likewise, many frog and chameleon species appear to be economically unsuited to breeding programs because of low reproductive success in captivity, and yet, Tensen noted, they "are being traded as pets in their thousands under the guise of captive breeding."

Even if traders could figure out how to breed all of the species people want as pets in captivity, not all conservationists think that they should. When Australian herpetologists Daniel Natusch and Jessica Lyons made a detailed investigation of the trade in green pythons from Indonesia, all supposedly from captive-bred stock, they found that many facilities did not actually know how to breed reptiles successfully. Some did not even have premises on which to attempt breeding. The researchers estimated that 80 percent of these snakes exported to the pet trade are in fact caught in the wild. But the wild-caught trade in green pythons appeared to be sustainable because of their abundance in the wild.

In such cases, Natusch says, the wild-caught trade may be better for conservation than captive breeding: "You can incentivize people to protect the habitat. If you can harvest these animals sustainably, you can have an income from the forest, and you don't have to cut down the forest."

Natusch, who works as a consultant to the IUCN, acknowledges that exporters can do horrible things for the trade—for instance, cramming snakes into suitcases and soda bottles to smuggle them through customs. He also agrees that taking snakes from endemic populations restricted to islands or outcrops can pose a threat to their survival. But the trouble with captive breeding, he notes, is that "once you take those animals from the wild, you have completely disassociated" the trade from any reason to care about the natural habitat. In contrast, he says, an entirely illegal trade in green pythons from Indonesia's Raja Ampat archipelago has motivated islanders to keep their forests intact. (A rare yellow color morph makes the snake trade there particularly lucrative.)

Demand and Supply

People who collect rare species are often "convinced they are doing wonderful things for animals" by taking them out of the wild and sheltering them from hunger, predation and other natural threats, says University of Oxford conservation biologist Tom P. Moorhouse, lead author of a 2017 study of consumer attitudes toward exotic pets published in *Conservation Letters*. He observes that buyers also typically assume "their ethical duties have been taken care of by the time an animal reaches the market." They have not. "We need a campaign to convince people that this isn't the case and that their choices have a massive effect," Moorhouse adds. "If there were no demand, no market for wild-caught exotics, there'd be no point paying someone to capture animals from the wild."

The pet industry has yet to come to terms with the issue of how the trade is affecting animal populations in the wild. Still, it does care about conservation, insists Mike Bober, president of the Pet Industry Joint Advisory Council. "We think that there is a place for wild-caught and captive-bred in most of these communities—the important thing being the methods used for collection," he says. "When the animals are collected sustainably, especially when they are collected by indigenous people who depend on that for their livelihood, we are proud of that. When they are collected badly, it is a direct problem for our industry. We rely on healthy ecosystems for healthy animals, and without healthy pets, there is no healthy pet trade."

But healthy ecosystems are vanishingly rare in the human era, and no adequate standards of sustainable collecting exist. Sooner or later pet lovers and the trade will need to face up to that reality and devise better ways of sourcing animals in a world where forests, oceans and other habitats are running empty.

Referenced

Wildlife Laundering through Breeding Farms: Illegal Harvest, Population Declines and a Means of Regulating the Trade of Green Pythons (Morelia viridis) from Indonesia. Jessica A. Lyons et al. in *Biological Conservation*, Vol. 144, No. 12, pages 3073–3081; December 2011.

Defaunation in the Anthropocene. Rodolfo Dirzo et al. in *Science*, Vol. 345, pages 401–406; July 25, 2014.

Using Market Data and Expert Opinion to Identify Overexploited Species in the Wild Bird Trade. J. Berton C. Harris et al. in *Biological Conservation*, Vol. 187, pages 51–60; July 2015.

Under What Circumstances Can Wildlife Farming Benefit Species Conservation? Laura Tensen in *Global Ecology and Conservation*, Vol. 6, pages 286–298; April 2016.

Do Not Publish. David Lindenmayer and Ben Scheele in *Science*, Vol. 356, pages 800–801; May 26, 2017.

Information Could Reduce Consumer Demand for Exotic Pets. Tom P. Moorhouse et al. in *Conservation Letters*, Vol. 10, No. 3, pages 337–345; May/June 2017.

About the Author

Richard Conniff is an award-winning science writer. His books include The Species Seekers: Heroes, Fools, and the Mad Pursuit of Life on Earth *(W. W. Norton, 2011).*

How Do We Prevent Pets from Becoming Exotic Invaders?

By Jim Daley

This summer a professional trapper caught an alligator in a lagoon in Chicago's Humboldt Park, following a weeklong search that drew crowds of onlookers and captured national headlines. Dubbed "Chance the Snapper," after a local hip-hop artist, the five-foot, three-inch reptile had likely been let loose by an unprepared pet owner, say experts at the Chicago Herpetological Society (CHS). This was no anomaly: pet gators have recently turned up in a backyard pool on Long Island, at a grocery store parking lot in suburban Pittsburgh (the fourth in that area since May), and again in Chicago.

Keeping a pet alligator is illegal in most U.S. states, but an underground market for these and other exotic animals is thriving—and contributing to the proliferation of invasive species in the U.S. and elsewhere. As online markets make it steadily easier to find unconventional pets such as alligators and monkeys, scientists and policy makers are grappling with how to stop the release of these animals in order to prevent new invasives from establishing themselves and threatening still more ecological havoc. New research suggests that simply banning such pets will not solve the problem and that a combination of education, amnesty programs, and fines might be a better approach. Many people who release pets may simply be unaware of the dangers—both to the ecosystem and the animals themselves—says Andrew Rhyne, a marine biologist at Roger Williams University who studies the aquarium fish trade. People may think a released animal is "living a happy, productive life. But the external environment is not a happy place for these animals to live, especially if they're not from the habitat they're being released into," he says. "The vast majority of [these] species suffer greatly and die out in the wild."

Exotics to Invasives

Owners sometimes release alligators, as well as other exotic pets such as snakes and certain varieties of aquarium fish, when they prove too big, aggressive, or otherwise difficult to handle. But unleashing them on a nonnative habitat risks letting them establish themselves as an invasive species that can disturb local ecosystems. According to one estimate, nearly 85 percent of the 140 nonnative reptiles and amphibians that disrupted food webs in Florida's coastal waters between the mid-19th century and 2010 are thought to have been introduced by the exotic pet trade.

A study published in June in *Frontiers in Ecology and the Environment* found this trade is already responsible for hundreds of nonnative and invasive species establishing themselves in locations around the world. Examples range from Burmese pythons—which can grow more than 15 feet long and dine on local wildlife in the Florida Everglades—to monk parakeets, whose bulky nests atop utility poles and power substations around the U.S. cause frequent fires and outages. And because of the growth of direct-to-consumer marketplaces on websites and social media, "the trade in exotic pets is a growing trend," both in terms of the number of individual animals and the variety of species kept, says study leader Julie Lockwood, a Rutgers University ecologist. "Together, those increase the chances that this market will lead to an invasion" of an exotic species, she says.

To date, the main way officials have tried to combat the problem is with laws that simply prohibit keeping certain categories of animals as pets. But the effectiveness of this approach is unclear. Even though Illinois has outlawed keeping crocodilians as pets for more than a decade, Chance is just one of many CHS has had to deal with this year alone, says its president Rich Crowley. He likens the problem to illegal fireworks, noting that bans on exotic pets are inconsistent from one state to the next. For Illinois residents, "there's still a supply that is readily available, legally, across the border" in Indiana, he says. "There are people out there who are willing to take the chance of skirting the law because the reward of keeping [these] animals is worth the risk."

New research published recently in *Biological Invasions* underscores this point, finding that banning the sale and possession of invasive exotic species in Spain did not reduce their release into urban lakes in and around Barcelona. "For these invasive species, legislation for the management of invasions comes too late," because they have already established themselves in the local environment, says University of Barcelona ecologist Alberto Maceda-Veiga, the report's lead author.

Phil Goss, president of the U.S. Association of Reptile Keepers, says that instead of blanket bans, he would like to see ways for responsible pet owners to still possess exotic species—with laws targeting the specific problem of releasing animals into the wild. "We're certainly not against all regulation," he says. "What we'd like to see is something that will punish actual irresponsible owners first rather than punishing all keepers as a whole."

Training and Tagging

Instead of bans, Maceda-Veiga's study recommends educating buyers of juvenile exotic animals about how large they will eventually grow and taking a permit-issuing approach that requires potential owners to seek training and accreditation. "You need a driving license to drive a car," and people should be similarly licensed to keep exotic pets, Maceda-Veiga says. He and his co-authors contend that licensing, combined with microchips that could be implanted in pets to identify owners, could curb illegal releases.

Rhyne agrees that giving buyers more information would likely help. "I think the education part is really important," he says. "We should not assume that the average consumer understands (a) how big the animal will get once it's an adult and (b) what the harm could be if it got out in the wild." Crowley concurs and says CHS has worked with municipal authorities to make sure pet owners who might have a crocodilian that is getting too big for the bathtub are referred to the organization for assistance. Also, some state agencies offer alternatives to dumping an animal in the wild that protect owners from legal repercussions. Lockwood says devising responsible ways for owners to relinquish such pets could help. But for this to work, "you need to make it as easy as possible" to turn in an animal, she says. In 2006 Florida's Fish and Wildlife Conservation Commission (FWC) established an amnesty program that allows owners to surrender their exotic pets with no questions asked. So far more than 6,500 animals have been turned over to the program, says Stephanie Krug, a nonnative-species education and outreach specialist at FWC. A few other states have followed Florida's lead in establishing amnesty initiatives.

Rhyne says some of the onus for controlling exotic animals should fall on the pet industry itself. "If you don't regulate yourself and make sure you're doing your best not to trade in species that are highly invasive, you're going to create a problem that [lawmakers] are going to fix for you," he adds. Mike Bober, president of the Pet Industry Joint Advisory Council, says the pet care community is considering ways to proactively address the problem. "We look at that being primarily based in education and partnership," he says.

As for what became of Chance, the erstwhile Windy City denizen is acclimating to his new home at the St. Augustine Alligator Farm Zoological Park in Florida. An aerial photograph of the Humboldt Park lagoon adorns his enclosure—but he is back where he belongs.

About the Author

Jim Daley is a freelance journalist from Chicago. He writes about science and health.

Why Pet Pigs Are More like Wolves Than Dogs

By Jason G. Goldman

I t's a classic television trope: Timmy has fallen down a well! Lassie can't save him herself, so she runs to find help. Actually, Timmy never did fall down a well in the entire run of the TV show. But the idea that a dog could seek help from a human does have a solid basis in science.

In what's known as the "unsolvable task" experiment, a dog first learns how to open a puzzle box with a tasty treat inside. The puzzle is then secretly switched for another that's impossible to solve. After becoming frustrated, dogs shift their attention away from the puzzle and onto a nearby human and then back to the puzzle. The dog attempts to shift the human's attention to the puzzle as a request for help. Human infants do the same thing. Such efforts are called "referential communication."

So if dogs behave this way, you might expect the same from their close relatives: wolves. But when researchers tested wolves raised by humans, the animals just kept trying to solve the puzzle, never seeking help. Since the dogs and wolves were all raised the same way and by the same people, domestication must be responsible for the behavior. So researchers began studying other domesticated creatures.

> "Other animal species—for example, horses, goats—have been tested in this test. But there were no direct comparisons with dogs."
>
> Paula Pérez Fraga, an ethologist at Eötvös Loránd University in Hungary.

Pet cats respond more like wolves than like dogs. Cats are domesticated, but they are not social like dogs and wolves. Pigs, however, are social.

"When pigs live in the wild—or even wild boars—these animals live in groups. They need to communicate with their conspecifics to be able to live."

Which is why the researchers decided to compare pet dogs with pet pigs. While the pigs revealed that they were capable of referential communication, they didn't actually turn to people for help. Once the task became unsolvable, they acted more like wolves, determined to find a solution on their own. The results were published in the journal *Animal Cognition*. [Paula Pérez Fraga et al., Who turns to the human? Companion pigs' and dogs' behaviour in the unsolvable task paradigm]

"What domestication means is literally that there's a genetic change in the animal, in the species from their wild relatives. And normally this genetic change has appeared because of human pressure."

Most domesticated animals, including dogs, cats, horses, goats, foxes, and so on, show similar anatomical and physiological changes associated with domestication. But Fraga says her study shows that the domestication process can proceed along different pathways in different animals. And that could explain why domestication and sociality alone can't explain why dogs react the way they do when faced with an unsolvable puzzle. Fraga thinks that it could be related to their domestication history.

"Their domestication was different. Pigs have been domesticated mostly for being a meat resource."

It was only later that we started treating some pigs as pets. Dogs, on the other hand, were treated as companion animals from almost the beginning—which appears to explain their willingness to ask for our help.

—Jason G. Goldman

[The above text is a transcript of this podcast.]

About the Author

Jason G. Goldman is a science journalist based in Los Angeles. He has written about animal behavior, wildlife biology, conservation, and ecology for Scientific American, Los Angeles *magazine, the* Washington Post, *the* Guardian, *the* BBC, Conservation *magazine, and elsewhere. He contributes to* Scientific American's *"60-Second Science" podcast, and is co-editor of* Science Blogging: The Essential Guide *(Yale University Press). He enjoys sharing his wildlife knowledge on television and on the radio, and often speaks to the public about wildlife and science communication.*

Online Reptile Trade Is a Free-for-All That Threatens Thousands of Species

By Rachel Nuwer

C ave geckos exemplify evolution at its most fantastic. Some have bloodred eyes and sport bright yellow bands down their dark body. Others are Popsicle blue or bear camouflagelike patterns of fiery orange and brown. Many species of these lizards are only found over a tiny range, such as a single limestone hill in China. More than a dozen are listed as threatened with extinction, some of them critically so, by the International Union for Conservation of Nature (IUCN).

Yet partly because they are rare and imperiled, cave geckos are all the rage among reptile collectors. They are among the nearly 4,000 reptile species—including highly endangered ones—that are routinely traded online, according to a paper published on Tuesday in *Nature Communications*. Animals from 90 percent of those species, representing half of the individual reptiles traded on the web, are captured from the wild, the authors found. And the majority of these species are not included in any international regulations meant to ensure their trade is sustainable. "At the moment, the status quo is that anything can be traded until you say it can't," says study co-author Alice Hughes, an ecologist at the Chinese Academy of Sciences. "This leaves thousands of species vulnerable to extinction."

As the new paper shows, no organization keeps track of global trade data for species that are not included in the Convention on International Trade in Endangered Species of Wild Fauna and Flora (CITES), a global treaty created in 1973 to ensure commerce involving wild species does not imperil them. Hughes was interested in determining how representative CITES is in terms of the international reptile trade, which affects snakes, lizards, turtles, tortoises, and crocodilians, among others. She and her colleagues compiled official data from 2000 to 2019 from CITES and U.S. Fish and Wildlife Service records and then gathered their own information from websites that sell reptiles. For the latter, they used an algorithm to identify and scrape the data from nearly 24,000 pages at 151 websites in English, German, Spanish, Japanese, and French.

The researchers tallied 3,943 species, or 36 percent of all known reptile species, for sale online. Most were those that are legal to trade as pets. But the question of whether a given species can be legally sold internationally is not automatically linked to its conservation status. More than a third of the reptiles on the list—including Borneo's earless monitor lizard and Madagascar's *Uroplatus finaritra*, a leaf-tailed gecko—have not been evaluated for their conservation status. This situation means scientists have no way of knowing if trade impacts those species' survival. Of the ones that have been evaluated, more than 500 are listed by the IUCN as in danger of extinction. That group includes more than 100 species that are critically endangered, such as Lauhachinda's cave gecko in Thailand and Yamashina's ground gecko in Japan.

The study's findings still underestimate the true number of reptile species caught up in trade, Hughes says, because its analysis did not include social media sites—where previous research has shown that high levels of wildlife trade take place. The paper also lacks results from websites in languages other than the five it considered.

Additionally, the research does not attempt to quantify how many individuals of each species are sold online, says Vincent Nijman, a wildlife trade expert at Oxford Brookes University in England, who was not involved in the study. "The paper highlights that, indeed, trade affects a very large number of species," he says. "But if you really want to change policy, you must have a more definite idea of the real volumes involved. That's not a criticism of this study, but that's ultimately where we have to go with future work."

Hughes and her colleagues found that 79 percent of reptile species sold online are not regulated by CITES. For those species and others that are not part of the treaty, quantities would likely be impossible to determine, Hughes says, because no agency tracks them.

To be included in CITES, species must go through a lengthy nomination process—one that, on average, takes more than 10 years to complete, according to a 2019 *Science* paper. Just showing that trade threatens a species is also not necessarily enough to warrant adding it to the treaty, because commercial interests often take precedence over science, conservationists have warned. "I attended the CITES conference last year in Geneva, and I was frankly stunned by how much of it seemed to be purely economically motivated," Hughes says.

The academic world perhaps "underestimates the overall cost of regulating species under CITES," the CITES Secretariat wrote in a statement to *Scientific American*. "It is probably true that the strong compliance mechanisms that CITES developed over the years, and for which it is feared and famous, have more impact if species are involved that are commercially important" for the relevant countries where those species are found.

John Scanlon, former secretary-general of CITES, who was not involved in the study, says he does not share the observation that the treaty's members often value economic considerations over scientific ones. Lesser known species of birds, insects, frogs, lizards, rodents, snakes, turtles, and more "do not make the headlines, like issues do with cheetah, giraffes, lions, elephants, and rhinos, but they do make up a majority of the listing proposals," he says. "CITES is imperfect, but it has proven to be quite effective."

That said, "there are clearly gaps in our knowledge and data on trade in unlisted species, including reptiles," Scanlon adds. "This report shows that parties should be proposing more reptiles for listing under CITES, which, on the face of this report, looks warranted."

Hughes questions whether the treaty is the best tool for quickly ensuring the pet trade does not imperil species, however. A more effective strategy, she says, would be for individual countries to pass legislation banning the import of certain wild-caught animals, as the U.S. and European Union have already done for many bird species. At the same time, the pet industry could transition to captive-breeding operations with necessary oversight. "We are not against keeping exotic animals as pets, but it has to be sustainable," Hughes says. "We need to develop better systems for making sure pet trade does not lead to species extinctions."

About the Author

Rachel Nuwer is a freelance science journalist and author who regularly contributes to Scientific American, *the* New York Times *and* National Geographic, *among other publications. Follow Nuwer on Twitter @RachelNuwer.*

New Vaccine Could Save Rabbits from Fatal Disease

By Tatum McConnell

Driving his car through a Tennessee ice storm in early February was a risk that veterinarian Logan Kopp knew he had to take. The reward: rescuing four vials containing 40 doses of a new vaccine for a highly contagious and fatal virus afflicting rabbits. A storm-related power outage had knocked out refrigeration at Priest Lake Veterinary Hospital in Nashville-Antioch, Tenn., threatening to degrade the vaccines doses in cold storage there.

Kopp managed to preserve the vials of vaccine by transferring them from his workplace to his home refrigerator. "It was pretty awful," he recalls of the treacherous drive, which took nearly six hours to complete in the storm. But he felt he had no other option.

The virus, known as RHDV2, causes rabbit hemorrhagic disease, a form of hepatitis. It is currently spreading through wild and domestic rabbit populations in the U.S., Mexico and beyond. The disease progresses rapidly and is fatal for up to 90 percent of infected rabbits. The virus spreads largely by contact among the animals and their body fluids. Surfaces, such as people's clothing, can also transmit it.

RHDV2 is not known to infect humans. But human movement of rabbits is likely a significant factor in the disease's spread, with geographically random cases popping up in domestic rabbits, says Bryan Richards, emerging disease coordinator at the National Wildlife Health Center in Madison, Wis.

Fortunately, as Easter approaches, things are looking up for at least some rabbits. In September 2021 the U.S. Department of Agriculture's Center for Veterinary Biologics granted emergency authorization for a vaccine against the disease. The following month a vaccine clinic appeared in California, where southern counties had experienced a wild outbreak of the virus. Rabbit owners' groups shared resources and information online about the resurgent virus and newly available vaccine. By this spring, more than 40 states and Washington, D.C., have access to the vaccine, according to the manufacturer Medgene Labs. A Web site serving rabbit owners lists more than 400 clinics and other sites offering RHDV2 vaccination. Many veterinary practices with vaccine in stock are reaching out to clients who own rabbits and are encouraging vaccination.

When Tennessee's first cases of rabbit hemorrhagic disease were confirmed in late January, Kopp knew the clock was ticking to protect the area's rabbits. The vaccine doses he saved during the storm were among the first Priest Lake Veterinary Hospital received.

That clinic has since vaccinated about 170 rabbits, 110 of them at a drive-through vaccination event hosted by the clinic in March. But there are a lot more rabbits out there: about 1.7 million households in the U.S. keep at least one as a pet, according to the American Pet Products Association. In some areas of the country, vaccine appointments are hard to find. One of Kopp's clients drove nine hours round trip to get her bunny vaccinated.

The virus is now endemic in 11 U.S. states, and cases have popped up in wild or domestic rabbits in 19 states over the past year, according to a frequently updated USDA map.

Estimates of population sizes of the country's predominant rabbit species—such as domestic rabbits, which are typically kept as pets, eastern cottontails, and species of jackrabbits—are difficult to obtain. As many as 3,500 riparian brush rabbits, an endangered species, live at the San Joaquin River National Wildlife Refuge, says Deana Clifford, a senior wildlife veterinarian at the California Department of Fish and Wildlife (CDFW).

Scientists are worried that RHDV2 could threaten the riparian brush rabbit population, along with other rare or endangered species of lagomorphs. A total of 24 rabbit species, or closely related species, worldwide are designated as endangered or vulnerable to extinction by the International Union for Conservation of Nature's Red List of Threatened Species. Since 2010 RHDV2 has caused outbreaks of rabbit hemorrhagic disease on five continents, according to a 2021 study published in *Transboundary and Emerging Diseases.*

The long-term impacts of the virus and its vaccine are unclear. Vaccination can save lives of pet rabbits. But trapping and vaccinating sufficient numbers of most wild rabbit species—at least 60 percent of a region's population—to control an outbreak can be challenging and costly, says Carlos Rouco Zufiaurre, an ecologist at the University of Córdoba in Spain. He explains that the vaccine's protection eventually wanes, which could enable viral spread to resume in groups of wild rabbits.

Nevertheless, CDFW and other partners have undertaken an effort to vaccinate the riparian brush rabbits at the San Joaquin River refuge. The team procured vaccines made in France, which were available under special conditions before the U.S.-produced vaccine. About 700 rabbits at the refuge have been vaccinated to date, Clifford says. "What we're trying to do is keep about 15 to 20 percent of the population vaccinated at any given time [so] that, if and when the disease ever comes to the refuge…, we don't lose them all," she adds.

Vaccines have also reached the endangered Columbia Basin pygmy rabbit, the smallest species in North America, under a recovery effort led by the Washington Department of Fish and Wildlife and the U.S. Fish and Wildlife Service. Clifford explains that while not all rabbits can be vaccinated, "in these special circumstances, we do think vaccination can have an impact."

The California outbreak, which also affected rabbits in the Southwest and Mexico, occurred from 2020 to 2021. The episode in those regions combined represents one of the largest recorded North American outbreaks of RHDV2, according to the 2021 *Transboundary and Emerging Diseases* study. The rapid spread of the virus was a surprise, says Andrea Mikolon, a veterinarian at the California Department of Food and Agriculture and a co-author of the study.

The outbreak first gained CDFW's attention in May, when biologists in the state found over a dozen dead black-tailed jackrabbits in the desert north of Palm Springs, says Clifford, who is also a co-author on the outbreak study. Into 2021 CDFW typically received citizen reports of one to five dead rabbits at a time, with occasional reports of large numbers of deaths.

No wild cases have been confirmed in California this year, but Clifford says the disease can spread undetected.

For now, the hope is that the campaign among veterinarians to vaccinate pet rabbits could slow the spread of RHDV2 in the U.S. Kopp takes time to speak with many clients, explaining that reliable clinical trials have shown the vaccine to be safe and effective. "There's definitely some excitement, but I think a lot of people are just nervous just because it's unknown," Kopp says. For now, he'll keep working to protect rabbits, one phone call and one vaccine at a time.

About the Author

Tatum McConnell is an environmental journalist based in New York City. Follow her on Twitter @tatum_mcconnell.

GLOSSARY

allele One of many forms a particular gene on a chromosome can take.

amalgam A combination or mixture.

anthropomorphize To describe a behavior in human terms without evidence; an error animal behavior researchers try to avoid.

atrophy To degrade or waste away.

biopsy A medical test involving the extraction of a tissue sample to check for disease.

conventional (linguistics) When a word or language pattern is specific to a language and culture, rather than universal to all languages.

contentious Controversial or up for debate.

correlation A statistical relationship between variables, regardless of whether it is causal.

demography The study of a given population, attempting to measure that population as well as other health, environmental, and social factors in it.

domestication The evolutionary and behavioral changes from a species' wild form to a form preferred by humans.

dysplasia The existence of abnormal cells in an organism, which may or may not be cancerous.

ethogram A record of the range of behavior types exhibited by an animal.

exacerbate To increase the severity of or make worse.

laterality Preference for one side of the body, as in "handedness" in humans.

minutia The small details of something.

mutually exclusive Describing two events or conditions that cannot take place simultaneously.

Neandertal A now-extinct early human subspecies; sometimes spelled Neanderthal.

olfactory Relating to scent and the scent organs.

repertoire A range of types of behavior one can exhibit.

selective advantage A feature of an organism that allows it to reproduce.

static Unmoving or unchanging.

stigma Negative reputation or social attitudes surrounding an attribute or activity.

supine Laying on one's back.

unequivocal Clear and unambiguous; inviting no other interpretations.

FURTHER INFORMATION

"Domestication Timeline," American Museum of Natural History. https://www.amnh.org/exhibitions/horse/domesticating-horses/domestication-timeline.

"The Power of Pets: Health Benefits of Human-Animal Interactions," National Institutes of Health. https://newsinhealth.nih.gov/2018/02/power-pets.

Goldman, Jason G. "Is Pedagogy Specific to Humans? Teaching in the Animal World." *Scientific American*, May 12, 2011, https://blogs.scientificamerican.com/thoughtful-animal/is-pedagogy-specific-to-humans-teaching-in-the-animal-world/.

Goldman, Jason G. "The Russian Fox Study," *Scientific American*, June 14, 2010, https://blogs.scientificamerican.com/thoughtful-animal/monday-pets-the-russian-fox-study/.

Lessmoellmann, Annette. "Can We Talk?" *Scientific American*, October 1, 2006, https://www.scientificamerican.com/article/can-we-talk/.

Pedrinelli, Vivian, et al. "Environmental Impact of Diets for Dogs and Cats," *Scientific Reports*, November 17, 2022, https://www.nature.com/articles/s41598-022-22631-0.

Platt, John R. "Illegal Pet Trade Threatens 13 Indonesian Birds With Extinction," *Scientific American*, May 25, 2016, https://blogs.scientificamerican.com/extinction-countdown/13-indonesian-birds/.

Simring, Karen Schrock. "What Your Pet Reveals About You," *Scientific American*, September 1, 2015, https://www.scientificamerican.com/article/what-your-pet-reveals-about-you1/.

CITATION

1.1 Why Do Cats Purr? By Leslie A. Lyons (April 3, 2006); 1.2 What You Don't Know About Your Dog's Nostrils By Julie Hecht (March 31, 2015); 1.3 Why Cats Taste No Sweets By David Biello (September 1, 2015); 1.4 How House Cats Evolved By Carlos A. Driscoll, Juliet Clutton-Brock, Andrew C. Kitchener, Stephen J. O'Brien (September 1, 2015); 1.5 Untangling the Mystery of How Fido Became Humankind's Best Friend By Jason G. Goldman (July 19, 2017); 1.6 What a Dog Geneticist Wants You to Know about Dog Genetics By Julie Hecht (April 25, 2018); 1.7 Good News for Dogs with Cancer By Amy Sutherland (December 30, 2019); 1.8 What Is a Dog Anyway? By Pat Shipman (December 8, 2022); 2.1 Wolves Have Local Howl Accents By Jason G. Goldman (April 5, 2016); 2.2 How Do Bonobos and Chimpanzees Talk to One Another? By Felicity Muth (November 5, 2016); 2.3 The First 'Google Translate' for Elephants Debuts By Rachel Nuwer (June 9, 2021); 2.4 'Chatty Turtles' Flip the Script on the Evolutionary Origins of Vocalization in Animals By Pakinam Amer (December 2, 2022); 2.5 How Scientists Are Using AI to Talk to Animals By Sophie Bushwick (February 7, 2023); 3.1 Many Animals Can Think Abstractly By Andrea Anderson (May 1, 2014); 3.2 We Are Not the Same (& That Is Fine): Different Approaches to Animal Behavior By DNLee (April 20, 2015); 3.3 Do Dogs Have Mirror Neurons? By Ádám Miklósi (March 1, 2016); 3.4 The World According to Dogs By Julie Hecht (May 1, 2017); 3.5 1 Sneeze, 1 Vote among African Wild Dogs By Jason G. Goldman (September 27, 2017); 3.6 New Research Questions "Pawedness" in Dogs By By Julie Hecht (March 31, 2018); 3.7 Small Dogs Aim High When They Pee By Julie Hecht (August 5, 2018); 4.1 Cuteness Inspires Aggression By Carrie Arnold (July 1, 2013); 4.2 We Surrender Our Dogs. Help Scientists Understand Why. By Julie Hecht (January 21, 2015); 4.3 Why So Many People Have Pets By Daisy Yuhas (September 1, 2015); 4.4 Good (and Bad) Ways to Help a Dog Afraid of Fireworks By Julie Hecht (June 30, 2017); 4.5 Culture Shapes How Children View the Natural World By Jason G. Goldman (April 1, 2018); 4.6 People With COVID Often Infect Their Pets By Frank Schubert (July 20, 2021); 4.7 Most Pets Can't Sweat: Here's What You Can Do for Them in a Heat Wave By Stella Marie Hombach (September 15, 2022); 5.1 What Is the Difference Between Hair and Fur? By Kate Wong (February 20, 2001); 5.2 Ferrets: Man's Other Best Friend By Jason G. Goldman (August 24, 2012); 5.3 Our Love of Exotic Pets Is Driving Wildlife Decline By Richard Conniff (October 1, 2017); 5.4 How Do We Prevent Pets From Becoming Exotic Invaders? By Jim Daley (October 7, 2019); 5.5 Why Pet Pigs Are More LIke Wolves Than Dogs By Jason G. Goldman (September 14, 2020); 5.6 Online Reptile Trade Is a Free-for-All That Threatens Thousands of Species By Rachel Nuwer (September 29, 2020); 5.7 New Vaccine Could Save Rabbits From Fatal Disease By Tatum McConnell (April 15, 2022).

Each author biography was accurate at the time the article was originally published.

INDEX